AFFILIATE MARKETING FOR BEGINNERS

12 STEPS TO YOUR AFFILIATE MARKETING BUSINESS IN 2021

SMM PUBLISHING

CONTENTS

❀ Created with Vellum

INTRODUCTION

Why you need to know about affiliate marketing and how to start making money from it.

Have you heard of the term affiliate marketing? You may be familiar with the term "affiliate marketing", and you may be totally clueless of what it actually means.

So many people often assume that affiliate marketing is a sort of pyramid scheme, well you must know that every online business seems like that at first. The advent of technology and the internet, in particular, has made so many impossibilities possible actually. Who would have ever thought that people could make thousands of dollars on the internet without having to leave the convenience of their homes? This "once upon a time" impossibility has actually been made possible over the years, through the advent of the internet. People are actually cashing out big-time online without leaving their homes.

One of such ways to make great money without having to leave your home is through Affiliate marketing. With affiliate marketing, you can actually become a salesperson without having your own product, you do not have to be bothered about how to deliver the products to the customers and you don't need to bother about how to develop or update the product. Basically, all you need to do is sell a product and get a commission for selling. The good news is, it doesn't even stop you from doing other things as well, you get to make money anywhere in the world.

What exactly is Affiliate marketing? Basically, Affiliate marketing has to do with finding a person of influence and a large follower-base, who would get a customized link to sell certain products at a particular commission. Every affiliate marketer has a particular link that's special when anybody buys using this link, the marketer gets a commission every time.

Over the years, online business has gained more prominence and become more popular. In order to sell your product to the right audience, using the traditional method of an advertisement doesn't work most times because it is only a waste of money and it targets at the general public instead of targeting the right audience. This is exactly why affiliate marketing was introduced by Amazon in 1996; in order to help you reach the right audience and also sell your product properly. There's a lot to learn about affiliate marketing, how it works and all the details. Do you want to join the list of people who are making cool cash from affiliate marketing? Do you have a community of people who trust you and have faith in your advice and recommendations? Come with me as I show you how to make money from all these as an affiliate marketer. There are dos and don'ts of affiliate marketing, you need to read this E-book to explore both the downsides and advantages of affiliate marketing.

CHAPTER ONE: WHAT IS AFFILIATE MARKETING?

Most people believe affiliate marketing is nothing but a Ponzi scheme but this belief isn't surprising, because we have a lot of people who still do not know how important affiliate marketing is.

We live in such a global world, and this is exactly why I find it extremely awkward to know that there are so many folks out there who are oblivious of the fact that y0u can make loads of money without leaving the convenience of your home.

Gone are those days when you had to wake up by the standard working hours to get yourself to work and get back home at the normal time, we live in an era where you do not need to conform to the old rules of *how to make money.* One of the most beautiful things in this world is having to make your money at your own pace, without leaving the comfort of your home and without having anyone boss you around for a few dollars. Although we all have been there, we all have plied that route but it is high time you woke up to the reality of this new ERA!

. . .

One of the various ways of making money online is AFFILIATE MARKETING. One of the most frequently asked questions about affiliate marketing is "*Is affiliate marketing a Ponzi scheme or a pyramid scheme*"? Well, if you are an average American, you should know that this question pops up every time something promises you so much when you basically have to invest little or nothing. You do not even have to live in America to have this notion, it is a popular belief which extends to even the coast of Africa- The belief that anything that promises so much when you have literally nothing to invest or little is a scam. In order to set this out there, you must know that AFFILIATE MARKETING IS NOT A PONZI. It is a legitimate way of making money without having to leave your home, by getting a certain commission for selling or advertising certain products.

While this the typical definition of affiliate marketing, affiliate marketing can further be broken down as a process which involves being a salesperson for a brand and earning a commission for doing your job as a salesperson. The only difference, in this case, is the fact that an affiliate marketer can actually work anywhere in the world. An affiliate marketer can represent a brand that's across the globe or far beyond the boundaries of your state or country.

Businesses who use affiliates often prefer people who resonate with the kind of audience they want to meet or reach. Most times, companies select affiliates with a large follower base: in order to be an affiliate, you must be able to reach a wide variety of people. This is why companies prefer influencers who have a community that trust them immensely. In order to sell a product to a large number of people, you must be connected with your audience in a way, they should be people who can trust you as well as your recommendations. Most affiliate marketers have a particular niche and these brands they advertise must have something related to their niche as well.

Every affiliate marketer has a unique link and a website when someone places an order using your special link to purchase a product, you get a commission for the sale of such products. Basically, anyone can be an affiliate and you are charged nothing to start your affiliate business.

Do you instantly become a billionaire as soon as you start your affiliate marketing business?

This is where so many people compare affiliate marketing to a pyramid scheme because of the fact that it has to do with the recruitment and referral of people to make money, the only difference here is that there is an actual product to sell. While affiliate marketing may sound easy and basic, you have to know that it isn't as easy as it sounds. There's a lot you must know in order to make your money as an affiliate marketer. The entire process of affiliate marketing is something that requires patience as well as hard work and consistency.

Why do companies prefer affiliate programs to the traditional method of advertising their products?

Unlike the traditional method of advertising your product, where you have to print flyers, use billboards, jingles and television to market your product, affiliate marketing affords you the opportunity to reach your right audience and specific audience. Several brands have a particular audience they want to reach; a diaper company targets expecting mothers and nursing mums, not college student and aspiring models. Likewise, a lipstick and make-over products company targets females within the age range of 15 and above. If you are a business organization without an audience, it is very difficult to track your sales. What affiliate marketing does is that it ensures that your affiliates have the right kind of audience for your brand and helps you sell your products faster. The traditional kind of advertisement is often aimed at the general public and it is hardly directed at the right audience.

Most people wonder if there are many brands that offer affiliate programs, you will be surprised to know that majority of our favourite brands have certain affiliate programs. Ranging from your telecommunication companies to your favourite cereal company, they all offer affiliate programs. All you need to do if you have an interest in joining any affiliate program is to search for one that is related to your niche. Google is always ready to answer your questions and you can always look up the available affiliate programs in your locality. Amazon is the biggest of all companies that offer affiliate programs.

So many people still do not know how much benefits to affiliate marketing has to offer. Most affiliates are happy with their job because they have no business creating a website of their own or having a product of their own. Since affiliate marketing has to do with getting a commission for the sale of other people's products, there's no need for you to have a company of your own or have a product of your own in order to be an affiliate marketer. All you have to do is literally partner with an existing brand in order to enhance the sale of their products, this is the scope of affiliate marketing and one of the best things about it.

Another thing is that affiliate marketing doesn't stop you from having other things that bring you money as well. It doesn't stop you from having a second business or working. If you have a job already, you do not have to quit your job in order to start affiliate marketing; you can always work as an affiliate as a side business, as long as you have an active data connection from anywhere in the world.

Another beautiful thing about affiliate marketing is the fact that you do not have to worry about delivering products to the customers, that is the business of the company. Your business is to market the product to the customers, you don't have to be concerned with the entire sales process. You also do need any capital to become an affiliate, unlike other businesses that require some amount of capital, affiliate marketing requires no upfront money at all.

Is affiliate marketing that simple? What exactly do you do as an affiliate? The first thing you must note here is the fact that no aspect of marketing is easy. In order to sell anything to people, you must have certain strategies. This doesn't exclude affiliate "marketing". Just like I mentioned earlier, as an affiliate, you must have a community of people who already have some level of trust in you. These are people who love to hear from you, look forward to reading from you and people who have a strong belief in your recommendations. All you have to do as an affiliate is to offer these people a piece of advice by recommending your "affiliate" product to them and telling them how this product can help solve their problems. In order to make them believe you, you may have to show them a video of how this product works and how they can benefit from such a product. Most times, you have to be creative when it comes to telling your community about these products, you want to gain their attention and ensure that they are not just entertained by your advert but you want to persuade them to click the link in your bio to make a purchase. All you have to do is copy your special link on your social media platforms and encourage your followers to purchase such products. You get your commission when anyone uses your link to make a purchase.

How can you market your products as an affiliate, if you have a large following on social media?

If you are someone who already has a large following on your social media platforms, marketing your products as an affiliate shouldn't be difficult at all. This is because you must have established some relationship with your followers in order to have such a large following. Since you must be someone who has some content on your platforms, you do not have to worry too much about marketing a product as an affiliate, all you have to do is make sure you do not change your method when advertising a product. Stay true to yourself, be original and be creative in your approach. You can come up with a creative video in order to advertise the product in an attractive manner, while being creative, make sure your message is passed across to your audience in a persuasive way. Remember that you do not have to stress things, do not lose your authenticity when advertising, your audience can always tell when you are trying to be someone else. Let them know you are willing to help them solve a problem and tell them why they should purchase such products. Do not make the mistake of selling a product that isn't related to your niche in any way. Your audience would know you are only trying to make money and not willing to help them if you tried selling something completely out of your niche. Another thing to remember when advertising a product to your community of followers is to ensure that your voice resonates through your advert, use whatever method your followers are familiar with, if you are fond of using humour, do not fail to do that. Let your audience hear and see "YOU" whenever you are trying to market a product, this is the best way you can sell a product to your audience because they have built trust with YOU and are probably buying a product because YOU are recommending it. This is why you have to remain yourself when trying to sell products as an affiliate.

Where can you paste your affiliate links? Your affiliate links can be pasted anywhere, ranging from your emails to your blog posts, YouTube, e-books to any social media platform at all. If you are someone who watches YouTube videos a lot, you would notice that most YOUTUBERS always have links for products used in their videos. Such people are reviewing such products and recommending the products to their viewers. If you have a large following on YouTube, you can easily paste your affiliate links there and review the products in your videos. For instance, as someone who does make-up tutorials on YouTube, if you have an affiliate program with any of the make-up companies, you can post your link on YouTube after showing your videos how effective such products are in your videos. If the product turns out well in your video, you can be sure that your viewers would rush to your link to make a purchase of such products. This method has been used by so many YouTubers and it sure works like magic. If you are a blogger, all you have to do as an affiliate is to include your affiliate link in your blog post after telling your audience how the product can help solve their problems in your blog post. This is one of the ways bloggers make their money; through affiliate marketing. All you have to do is to ensure your blog post is captivating enough to grab the attention of your audience. These affiliate links can be pasted in review articles as well. You can also post on your social media platforms such as Facebook, WhatsApp, Instagram, LinkedIn, etc. Instagram allows you to post links in your bio alone and you can make videos or share pictures with captions telling your audience to click the link in your bio to make a purchase of such products.

Sometimes you may wonder why you aren't getting credit for every order that gets placed using your link, sometimes, you may not get credit for certain orders even if such orders are made with your affiliate links. The reason is that some people may place an order using your affiliate link, if this order is placed with a certain browser like chrome but the person buys using another browser like Firefox, you may not get credit for it and you may get no commission as well. Also if a cookie is placed when someone clicks your affiliate link but this person buys using another person's link, you will not get credit for it because the person bought using another person's affiliate link to make a purchase.

SUMMARY

Affiliate marketing can be defined as the act of promoting a company's product or another person's product, using a special link and website which can be pasted anywhere, in order to get some commission as soon as a purchase is made.

Anyone can be an affiliate marketer as long as you can reach lots of people. Although affiliate marketing seems basic, there are certain things that should be put in place.

Affiliate marketing affords you the opportunity to work from anywhere in the world as long as there is an internet connection.

Most people assume affiliate marketing is either a Ponzi or a pyramid scheme because it requires no money and promises so much. None of these is true, affiliate marketing is a legitimate method of earning money that has helped so many people become really wealthy.

The benefits of affiliate marketing include the fact that you do not have to be involved in the entire sales process and the fact that it requires no capital at all.

Your affiliate links can be pasted on YouTube and any social media platform.

In order to advertise your affiliate products as someone who already has a community of followers who trust your recommendations, you must be original and you must ensure your voice resonates with your followers while marketing your affiliate products.

CHAPTER TWO: HISTORY OF AFFILIATE MARKETING

Not everyone knows the history of affiliate marketing. Some people don't even care to know, there are so many things we find really important; things we can barely do without but no one cares to know how long such things have been in existence. Just like we wonder who was the first man who started certain things, I don't know about you but so many times when I have nothing important doing, I simply put on my thinking cap and ask questions like who was the first man to kick a ball? How did we start eating with a spoon? Who came up with that? Some of these questions are born out of mere inquisition and a desire to want to know the origin of certain things. While some of these questions may sound crazy or unnecessary, they are important in a way. They help you realize where you are coming from and tell you how much advancement we have today. This is why you must know that affiliate marketing started long ago.

Most people often assume that affiliate marketing came with the birth of the internet but no, affiliate marketing has been in existence for a very long time. Most people think affiliate marketing is simply making a purchase with a certain link and the owner of the link gets paid some money for referring a customer, but this isn't just what affiliate marketing is. Affiliate marketing as a concept started when my great grandfather's mechanic would pay my great grandfather some discount for bringing him a new customer. Well, it's not important to know who my great grandfather is or the name of his mechanic. The idea I'm trying to give here is that the concept of affiliate marketing started when people would get paid for referring a new customer to sellers or people rendering certain services. This is basically the concept of affiliate marketing and it has been in existence for a very long time.

Many years back, no one would have thought that people would be meeting other people from different parts of the world with just a few clicks? The idea of connecting with people who live beyond your geographical area would have seemed like an impossible one 100 years ago. However, we now live in an era where you can meet with people across the globe, sell things to them, start a relationship with them and even get married to them. Several people have found partners through the internet, people have met their spouses who are based in other countries on the internet. This is how much advancement we have had in the past few years. The invention of the Internet has increased and improved our lives in so many ways. Our businesses are not left out of this advancement and improvement, you can easily ship your products worldwide with the birth of the internet. You can buy and sell goods from anywhere in the world without leaving the convenience of your home.

When selling your products to people, it is necessary to know where most of your customers are coming from and how they got to know about you. This is easier tracked using the internet, you can know who your customers are, what they like and this can even help you increase your sales. All these have led to the improvement of affiliate marketing.

Originally, the origin of affiliate marketing can be traced to a man named William Tobin in 1989. Williams Tobin set up an affiliate program for his company PC Flowers and gifts in the year 1989. This man set the pace for affiliate marketing back then. Although what we have as modern affiliate marketing is a lot different from what we used to have back then, the general idea of affiliate marketing has barely changed a bit.

If we have to thank anyone for making affiliate marketing available to the general public, we have Amazon to thank for bringing affiliate marketing closer to everyone in the year 1996. Ever since the inception of affiliate marketing in the year 1996, it has continued to thrive and as indeed remained an amazing way to make money.

The invention of cookies has also helped the promotion of affiliate marketing a whole lot. Cookies were invented to help you know what users are doing and how they are responding to certain websites. Cookies help to track what the users are doing; they are tiny pieces of data which are kept in every user's browser. If you make use of the internet really well which I'm sure you do, you wouldn't be reading this book if you weren't an internet user, you must have noticed a pop up that tells you that this website uses cookies. You may be wondering why they are called "cookies", a certain web programmer named Lou Montulli named cookies after "magic cookies". Cookies are basically used by third parties to know how the information on a website is being used and how they can tell what works for a website and what doesn't work. This has helped people improve their websites and attend more to the customer's needs.

In the year 1998, two amazing affiliate networks came up with the idea of bringing affiliate marketing closer to smaller businesses who aren't a part of amazon. When discussing affiliate marketing, it would be really wrong to not mention Click bank and Commission, as they have helped the concept of affiliate marketing. Till date, we still have very few affiliate networks and click bank is still a very relevant affiliate network. What they do basically is to make affiliate marketing programs available to small businesses while charging a fee from them. These small businesses then look for people with the right audience to help them market their products by offering them some commission in return.

Skim links is also a very notable feature we mustn't hesitate to talk about when discussing the history of affiliate marketing. Skim links was launched in the year 2007 and was brought into the global picture, for the sole purpose of helping publishers make use of affiliate marketing for the generation of essential commerce revenue by writing contents for certain products.

You must know that so many publishers have made great revenue from Skim links and it has remained one of the best ways to make money as a publisher, ever since it was launched in 2007. Affiliate marketing has really come a long way and has remained even more efficient over the years.

. . .

In the U. K alone, it was recorded that affiliate networks had made about £2.16 billion in the year 2oo6. There was also a record which stated that the worldwide revenues from affiliate marketing as at the year 2006 was $6.5 billion.

Affiliate marketing keeps waxing stronger till date. Although it has become slightly different from the way it used to be back then, it only seems to be evolving. There is no sign that affiliate marketing may cease to be in existence anytime soon, this is because a lot of people are still benefitting greatly from the concept of affiliate marketing.

CHAPTER THREE: BENEFITS OF AFFILIATE MARKETING

While explaining the concept of affiliate marketing in chapter one, I already mentioned some of the benefits of affiliate marketing. However, there is a great need to know that there are numerous benefits that come with affiliate marketing and it is essential to explore some of these benefits in order to heighten your interest in the subject of affiliate marketing.

If you are someone who is familiar with the frenzy of the recent "online business", you should be able to reel off the benefits of some of these online sources of income. Aside from the glaring fact that affiliate marketing affords you an opportunity to make money without having to leave your home, there are other benefits you need to know as well. Are you wondering what these benefits are? Then let's get to business already; You must note that affiliate marketing offers several benefits to both the affiliates and the businesses alike. Some of these benefits are as follows:

. . .

It is a great way to make passive income: One great benefit of affiliate marketing is the fact that you can make passive income from it. The mantra of every individual who is interested in investing is "make money while sleeping". This mantra has worked for people involved in affiliate marketing as well. If you are thinking of something that affords you an opportunity to make money even without your direct presence; when you are far away on a romantic holiday with your partner, the last thing you want to think about is "work", this is one of the best times you want something that still gives you money even when you aren't actually working. Affiliate marketing can help your dream come true. Since your affiliate links are pasted everywhere already, the only thing you have to do is relax and remain patient while your money is being made even when you are literally sleeping. Everyone genuinely wants to build a passive income, I personally believe in the theory of earning a passive income, it's one of the 99 ways to become a billionaire. Don't worry about the 98 other ways to become a billionaire, concentrate on affiliate marketing.

It is extremely lucrative: If there is a benefit of affiliate marketing that cannot be overemphasized, it is the fact that it is extremely lucrative. Are you thinking of doing something that can bring you lots of money in no time? Well, have you heard of affiliate marketing? It is a great way to make lots of money as long as you are patient, consistent and hard working. The industry of affiliate marketing itself is a billion-dollar industry itself. You can imagine getting into such an industry and knowing just the right buttons to push. Before you know it, your dreams are falling into places before your own naked eyes and you are made for life. The world keeps getting even more digitalized than we can imagine and human beings keep getting even more insatiable, there are so many beautiful things in the world and I don't know anyone who doesn't crave comfort and a life of luxury. Sadly, the kind of life most people want can hardly be achieved by doing a 9-5 job. In order to make the kind of money you want, it is advisable to either go into a business like an affiliate marketing as a side business or a full-time deal. You will make money either ways.

It expands your knowledge: One other great benefit of affiliate marketing is the fact that it allows you to become really knowledgeable. There's something about affiliate marketing that makes you want to stay at the top of your game. You want to be really informed to know what's going on in the online world and how to call your shots in the affiliate marketing world, what this "desire to know" does to you is the fact that it increases your knowledge in all ways, it also exposes you to things you didn't know before. You get to know a whole lot about marketing and how to sell to a wide variety of people.

It is a low-cost business: One other great benefit of affiliate marketing is the fact that it is a business that comes with minimal cost. Most times when we are struggling with our finances, we all think about diversifying our income; doing a side business, the only thing that makes these thoughts disappear is lack of sufficient capital. There is virtually no business you want to do that doesn't require capital. This is one advantage affiliate marketing has over other types of business. The fact that it doesn't require any capital, you don't need to get yourself worked up over how to raise your capital. Affiliate marketing is a business that cuts across several niches and it is made available to various people regardless of your sex or race. It is absolutely free!

. . .

There is virtually no expertise required: Unlike other businesses that require some level of expertise, affiliate marketing is a kind of business that allows you to learn when you are already involved in the process. What's more beautiful than a business that requires no certificates or degree? Awesome right! Affiliate marketing is open to you regardless of the fact that you have little or no qualifications. Over the years there's been a great craze for "expertise" and "experience" in the labour market. It is either this company wants a person who has about 3-years-experience in something, or that company wants somebody who has 6-years-experience in another thing. The need for experience is really tiring and it often puts a lot of people off when job hunting. Unlike other businesses, affiliate marketing isn't one of those that require any level of expertise. It is basically open to everyone and anyone.

It is an awesome side business: One amazing benefit of affiliate marketing is the fact that it doesn't stop you from doing other things. You can still keep your job even as an affiliate and you still have enough time to focus on your affiliate marketing. Affiliate marketing doesn't stop you from doing two or more things at a time, you can always make time for other things as an affiliate marketer.

It isn't Rigid in any way: Affiliate marketing is something that can be done at any time and anywhere at all. All that is required is an active internet connection and a willingness to work. If you happen to be one of those people who crave independence in their work, affiliate marketing is a great option. You are the one who calls the shots in your work at your own time and your own convenience. It's just like being a freelancer, you are free to work at any time you desire and you may even decide to not work if you decide not to or if you do not feel like it. You do not have to resume work at any specified time as an affiliate, you do not have to deal with an annoying boss who nags or complains about anything and everything at all. You get to work on your own terms.

You are provided with the necessary marketing kit: Another benefit of affiliate marketing is the fact that you do not have to worry about having the necessary marketing kit. The company whose brand or product you are promoting provides you with the right marketing kit as at when you need it.

It makes you a marketing guru: One other benefit which affiliate marketing offers is the fact that you can become a marketing guru. Affiliate marketing helps you become aware of the numerous marketing strategies available. This means that you can become an effective marketer even when you decide to go into any kind of business. People who have great marketing strategies can basically survive anywhere and in any sector. It becomes easy to sell your own products when you finally decide to have one.

It is performance-based: This is one benefit which affiliate marketing offers to the companies offering the affiliate programs. The concept of affiliate marketing only ensures that an affiliate gets paid as soon as a cookie is placed using the affiliate's link. This ensures that the affiliates work so hard in other to ensure several orders are placed, using their own special link. This is a win-win situation for all! The company only pays when a product has been sold and the affiliate wants to ensure that the products are sold so as to get paid as well. This is why we say that affiliate marketing is performance-based; the affiliate only pays when there is a visible performance which is the placing of cookies when products are purchased.

. . .

You gain the trust of several people as a business: One benefit which affiliate marketing offers you as a business is a fact that you gain the trust of several people out there, by involving third parties. Most people who make purchases using an affiliate's link often do so because they trust the affiliate's recommendations. Therefore, by using affiliates, you make people trust your products as well.

You can generate more traffic: Another benefit which affiliate marketing offers businesses is the fact that you can generate more traffic on your website when people visit your website using various affiliate links. This is one reason every business should consider affiliate marketing as it can help you convert the massive traffic on your website to potential customers.

Your earnings are unlimited: Unlike every typical 9-5 job where you get paid for your time and not the value you offer; affiliate marketing helps you make money according to the values your offer. You can earn a lot from affiliate marketing in the space of only 24 hours. However, with a 9-5 kind of job, your boss only pays you the same amount at the end of the month, regardless of the fact that you really worked hard this week. Your pay remains exactly the same. However, with affiliate marketing, you get paid a certain commission per purchase. If you get people to make 50 purchases in one day, using your affiliate link, you get paid you commission for the 50 purchases made.

It ensures job security: We live in an era where there's no such thing as job security. Thousands of people apply for the same kind of job and when you end up being the lucky one who gets the job, you may be laid off from work anytime. With affiliate marketing, there is a security that comes with your job, you are the one who decides if you are tired of making money, this is when you may decide to stop. However, there's no such thing as getting laid off from work in affiliate marketing, if you have any problem

There is a sense of fulfilment that comes with affiliate marketing: While this may sound completely overrated to you, affiliate marketing can help you find fulfilment as a person. There are several individuals out there who are only into certain jobs because they have to make ends meet. This is why so many people live an unsatisfied life because they aren't pleased with the way they are going about life. Sometimes, the payment that comes with certain jobs is not even worth it in any way. However, most people keep going to work grudgingly and return the same way because they are not fulfilled with the kind of job they have. Affiliate marketing isn't a job that leaves you tired, exhausted and unfulfilled. Apart from the income that comes with it, it is a job that lets you explore your passion. Since there are several types of a niche in affiliate marketing, you can always find something that catches your fancy. There is basically a market for every niche out there; this makes you feel like you are making money by doing exactly what you love doing. This helps you feel really fulfilled within yourself.

SUMMARY

It helps you to make passive income

It is a great avenue to make money

It requires little or no cost

There is basically no expertise required

It can serve as a great supplementary source of income

It is completely flexible and independent

You are provided with your own marketing kit

You become a marketing guru

It helps you gain traffic and helps you gain the trust of people as a business

CHAPTER FOUR: WHAT DO YOU HAVE TO DO AS AN AFFILIATE?

Most affiliate marketers have unique strategies which they use. If you desire to be an affiliate, there are certain things you have to put in place. Some of these things include having the right mindset, a noticeable and very strong online presence and so on. You do not just wake up one morning to start affiliate marketing without knowing where to start from or without knowing exactly what you have to do. There's a need to do these necessary things in the correct manner in order to get your desired result and earn great money from affiliate marketing.

Here's a list of things you have to do as an affiliate marketer:

You need to have the right mindset: One important thing you have to do as an affiliate is to develop the right mindset. What kind of mindset are we talking about here? You must teach yourself to accept that although affiliate marketing is a very lucrative job, you still need to put in some hard work and the right consistency needed to survive as an affiliate marketer. Understand the fact that affiliate marketing isn't a get-rich scheme, it is a legitimate way of making money and like every typical legitimate business, you need to work hard. Although affiliate marketing doesn't require a lot of hard work like other businesses, with a mindset to be hard-working, you will make all you want with the right consistency, hard work and patience. This is why it is essential to develop the right mindset if you ever want to work as an affiliate.

You must have a blogging website: This is a requirement if you want to be a successful affiliate marketer. Why should you have a blogging website? Since Affiliate marketing has to do with selling certain products to a lot of people in order to make your money, having a blogging website would definitely help you reach more people faster, you can write articles reviewing the products and also leave your affiliate links in the articles. Creating a website has been made easy with the advent of WordPress. Most people who have made a fortune from affiliate marketing are those who have an active blogging website, where they regularly post articles about the affiliate products they are promoting. This is why you must have a blogging website.

Email auto-responders: One thing you also have to do as an affiliate marketer is that you must have a long list of e-mails. It is necessary to have the personal information of your audience. Having their emails is a great way to begin, you can keep them informed about any latest information about your affiliate products by sending messages to their mails; it's a great way to reach your audience personally.

Be completely honest: This is one thing you have to do as an affiliate marketer. Do not recommend a product if you don't have a clear idea of how such product works. The last thing you want is to throw away the trust people have in you. Regardless of how much you have to gain from promoting your affiliate products, it is best to tell your audience if there are downsides to the product you are promoting. You have to ensure the safety of your audience comes first before any other thing. You do not want them to lose their trust in you as this would cost you much more than you can imagine. You do not need to sugarcoat your affiliate products when advertising to your audience, you can be creative in your advert but you have to tell the honest truth. They would be really disappointed if they found out that you had only made them buy the products for your own pocket. In order to avoid this, an affiliate who wants to be successful has to ensure that nothing is sugarcoated.

You need to have a great online presence: If you are someone who likes staying off the cyber walls, affiliate marketing is certainly not for you. A successful affiliate marketer isn't just a faceless person, to be successful as an affiliate marketer you must be actively present online. Affiliate marketing is one of the greatest online businesses and if you want to really make money from it, you must have a great level of influence. You need to be able to influence the minds of people to purchase your affiliate products through your affiliate link so as to earn a great income from the business. There is no way you can be successful with affiliate marketing without a notable online presence.

Communicate with your audience: One thing every affiliate should know is the importance of communication. Remember that affiliate marketing needs the attention of your audience, you need to maintain regular communication with them so as to ensure that they click your link to make a purchase of the affiliate products. How can you foster communication with your audience as an affiliate marketer? You must be ready to let your audience in on all the details connected with a certain product; the pros, the cons and the exact way to go about using such products. This is because your audience needs to be convinced that they aren't making a mistake by buying such products. Tell them how this product can solve their problems and be ready to answer any question they may have about the products. It doesn't matter how unnecessary their questions are; you have to answer them regardless. In every business, communication is essential for a successful and smooth trade, affiliate marketing is one of such businesses.

You have to know the right affiliate programs to join: This is a very crucial one. The worst mistake you could make is joining an affiliate program that's totally wrong. Although we will still talk about this later in this book, it is essential for you to consider the legitimacy of an affiliate program before joining. You have to do your findings really well before joining any affiliate program, this is because there are several illegitimate affiliate programs out there. How can you determine the legitimacy of an affiliate program? Aside from doing your homework very well when it comes to any affiliate program, another way to know if an affiliate program is a scam is by confirming if there's any payment required for joining the affiliate program. Most affiliate programs require no payment at all, it is possible that any affiliate program that requires you to pay before joining isn't a legitimate one. You must also ensure that the affiliate program you are joining isn't a different niche from yours. One beautiful thing about affiliate marketing is the fact that there is a program for virtually every niche you can think of out there. Going for an affiliate program that's completely out of your niche is a wrong move as you may end up confusing your audience. Remember that your audience must have the impression that you are trying to help them find a solution to their problems. Joining an affiliate that has nothing to do with your niche wouldn't solve the problem of your audience and it may be difficult to promote such products. In order to avoid this, you must ensure the affiliate program you are joining has something to do with your niche. Another thing you have to consider is the commission rate which an affiliate program has to offer. You should go for affiliate programs that offer a great commission rate. There are affiliate programs that offer 30% commission and there are others that offer less or more, you have to go for programs with huge commission rate as such programs would help you make great money in no time. Another thing you must also consider when choosing affiliate programs is the payment method. Different affiliate programs use different payment methods; you have to ensure that the payment method involved in an affiliate program is available in your country before joining such a program. There are also certain limitations in some affiliate programs, you have to ensure you are comfortable with such limitations before signing up to join such programs.

Sell what you know: This still boils down to the fact that you shouldn't choose an affiliate program outside your niche. It is essential to sell only what you know. Although the saying "Sell what you know" is an old saying, it still works till date. The best way to profit or succeed in any business is to ensure you are selling only what you know about and not something you are totally clueless about.

. . .

Do not forget to add your affiliate links in your content every time: If you are someone who is quite familiar with the internet, you must have seen a blog or an article that reviews a product in details, with a link that lands you on the website where you can purchase such product. This is exactly something you shouldn't forget to do, take advantage of every opportunity you get to market your affiliate products by adding your affiliate link in your content.

Use Google Analytics: Since it is a little difficult to know how much you have made with an affiliate program, the best way to track your website in order to determine what's working and what's not working is by using Analytics. Google Analytics helps you determine how many visitors you get, where these people are coming from and what these people look like. You can also know how your blog posts are doing by using analytics. You can tell which of your post gets the most visitors and why. This helps you know if you should be making posts like that and helps you determine what your audience doesn't like. It is really necessary and essential to check your growth as an affiliate from time to time with google analytics.

CHAPTER FIVE: QUESTIONS YOU WANT TO ASK AS AN AFFILIATE

In order to cut your teeth as an affiliate marketer, it is really necessary for you to ask certain questions. These questions keep you on track and help you define your goals in affiliate marketing. Every business requires a certain degree of strategy. If you want to be successful with business, there is a necessity to be strategic and the only way to determine if you are 0n track is to ask intelligent questions. When we attain a certain age in life, we feel like we should have known everything and we sometimes get scared of asking questions. This is the only reason why so many people fail and make mistakes. Now, technology has made everything relatively easy, as long as you have your mobile phone with you, you can ask as many questions as possible, Google is always ready to answer your questions, no matter how ridiculous they are.

Imagine travelling to a place you have never been to before? Imagine a scenario where you have no access to a google map. In a situation like this, you need to ask questions if you do not want to end up missing your way. The need to ask questions cannot be overemphasized. When we were born, we were born with a great curiosity to "know." A child would want to know if the story of the fairy tooth was true and if mermaids were real. While deviating from the main topic here, the point is that you need to ask as many questions as possible if you do not want to make mistakes in affiliate marketing. You would never get arrested or reprimanded for asking too many questions. In case you are clueless of the right questions you should ask, here's a list of questions you need to ask as an affiliate marketer:

What do you want to achieve with affiliate marketing: It is very important to have your goals defined? You have to know exactly what you want to achieve as an affiliate marketer. Know what you want and stick to what you want exactly. For instance, you may decide to go into affiliate marketing in order to know how it works. Money isn't always the priority. Know exactly what you want from affiliate marketing as it would help you stick to your goals better. If You want to become an affiliate marketer just to know exactly how everything works, you must ensure you go for a program that lets you explore all you need to explore in the field. On the other hand, if what you want to achieve with affiliate marketing is "traffic" to your website, then you must stick to this goal as well in order not to deviate from your original goal. If what you want from affiliate is an avenue to make money, define your goal as well and go for affiliate programs that offer a great commission rate. You must also know what you want from your audience. This is where you have to make effective use of the CTA tactic (Call to Action). Let your audience know if you want them to click on your link to make purchases or you only want them to refer their friends. Let them know exactly what you want from them by clearly stating out your objective in your content.

. . .

Who are you selling to One thing I have come to realize in marketing is the fact that different people feel convenient selling to different target audiences. Have you found the target audience you are comfortable working with yet? Some people find it easy to sell to teenagers while some people find they do better with women or men. Know exactly who your target audience is and ensure that your message and content resonate with them every time. If your target audience cannot relate with your content and if your language doesn't capture your audience, it will be a little difficult to sell to them. The rule is to know exactly who you are selling to, what they want and the kind of mindset they have. If you have to sell to a set of people, it is important to know how their mind works. Put yourself in their shoes to ensure you can relate with them and know exactly what they would want in order to let them know you are on the same page with them. Affiliate marketing has a lot to do with solving the problems of your audience and making them realize you can solve their problem, the best way to do this is to know your audience enough to know what captivates them and what appeals to them.

Who do you want to work with: This is a question really important in affiliate marketing. You must have a clear niche that shows exactly what you love doing. In other words, you have to ensure you have a particular niche where you really want to work. Your niche is something your heart beats for, it helps you choose a field where you would work even if you weren't getting paid for your work. When your niche is already clear and you know exactly where you want to work, it would be easy to know what affiliate program you want to join. There's an affiliate program for virtually every niche you can think of and Amazon has so many of such programs. It would be really easy for you to choose an affiliate program as long as you already know what niche you want to work with.

How are you different? This is another essential question right here. You must know that the affiliate marketing industry is quite a competitive one. Since there are so many people doing the same thing with you, it is necessary for you to ask yourself if you are doing anything differently. What difference are you making in the industry and how creative are you in doing what you are doing. When you find yourself in an industry as competitive as the affiliate marketing industry, it is important for you to do something different from everyone. You have to be creative in your approach and also have to ensure that your content is an exceptional one, in order to be successful and have an edge over most of the people in the industry.

Why should your audience listen to you: It is important to ask this question as well.

Most people who have the attention of a great audience are those who are doing something spectacular. People just don't pay attention unless there's a reason to. Every influencer on social media is obviously been followed because they have "content". If you want your audience to listen to you, you must be able to deliver great content to them and you must also have something unique to offer. Think of something you love about someone who's influenced your life positively. What exactly do you like about them and how do they inspire you? Draw from their inspiration and ensure your audience get something like that from you. Aside from this, your audience is more likely to listen to you if you appear really confident about something. Confidence is an attractive quality and anyone can identify confidence when they see it. When writing product reviews or blog posts advising your audience to purchase a particular product, it is very important for them to see how confident you are about a product. They would definitely trust your recommendations if you are confident in your approach. Another reason your audience would listen to you is by showing them they can trust your recommendations. Most people would only listen to you if they can trust you, a certain study revealed that most women would only purchase skincare products if they had faith in the person selling or recommending to them. You can do this by showing them that they would never regret making the decision to purchase a product. These are ways to get your audience to listen to you.

These are questions you need to ask as an affiliate marketer. There are questions every business considering getting an affiliate marketer should ask as well. These questions are important because the last thing you want is to have the reputation of your brand soiled by taking on an affiliate marketer whose website may soil your brand. Although no one pays attention to brand reputation, people keep saying these are what matter; the sales, traffic and lead generation. However, you still have to remember that you do not need to partner with an affiliate whose website would be demeaning to your business in any way. The following are questions you need to ask an affiliate marketer before consenting to a partnership with them.

What are you bringing to the table: While this is a very obvious question, it is still important to be very clear and the best way to know what to expect is to ask questions. Most people would say they would give you more “sales”. Well, that’s often the most important thing but it is still necessary to discuss what your goal is with your affiliate. Do you need more sales? More traffic? Lead generation or you need to build trust with the members of the public? Whatever goals you have should be discussed with the affiliates to ensure they are on the same page with you. Tell them the kind of impression you are willing to give the general public about your brand. Remember affiliate marketers help to project the image of your company to the outside world? You need to ensure they are projecting the exact image you want them to project out there. We have seen affiliate marketers who market other people's brands like theirs, they project a beautiful image of the company and ensure that the impression everyone has about the company is an excellent one. It is important to ask your affiliates how they are willing to advance the development of your company and how they plan to go about it even if it means you have to increase the commission you are paying them. What matters is that your company's image is projected in the right way and it is also important that the general public gets the right message.

How would this affiliate's site reflect on my brand: Just like I mentioned, it is crucial to pay attention to your reputation as a brand. You have to know what kind of content the website puts out there. Does the website have anything in common with your website? Will the website reach the right audience? In order to determine if the website would reach your target audience, you need to ensure that the affiliate marketer works within your business niche. This is to ensure that your affiliate reaches the right audience you want to reach. You should also consider the kind of language and message which the affiliate marketer promotes on their website, ensure that the content resonates with your audience and the language is suitable for your target audience. This is to promote and project a perfect image of your brand to the general public.

How does the affiliate promote other brands: This question is very essential to a business seeking to choose an effective affiliate marketer. When you get to know how an affiliate promotes other brands on their website by checking out their website, you get to know if that's exactly how you want your brand to be promoted as well. Most affiliates often promote brands according to the commission rates they get from such brands. Checking out how they promote other brands helps you determine if you want to partner with such affiliates or not.

SUMMARY

In this chapter, we discussed the important questions you need to ask as an affiliate marketer as well as the questions necessary to ask when selecting affiliate marketers.

As an affiliate marketer, it is necessary to ask the following questions:

What you want to achieve with affiliate marketing
Who you are selling to
Who you want to work with
How are you different
Why your audience should listen to you

. . .

Before choosing an affiliate, you should ask the following questions:

You need to know what the affiliate is bringing to the table

How would the site reflect on your brand?

How does the affiliate promote other brands?

CHAPTER SIX: HOW TO CHOOSE THE RIGHT AFFILIATE PROGRAM?

Choosing the perfect affiliate program is often a daunting task but when you have the right knowledge and how to go about it the right manner, you can be sure to partner with a beautiful brand. Here's all you need to ensure that your affiliate marketing ride is nothing but awesome and super amazing. When you are already equipped with the necessary knowledge on how to choose an affiliate program, you can even begin to nurture other people who are upcoming affiliate marketers. We have had people who joined affiliate programs that ended up being an unpleasant program while we've also had people who became affiliates of brands that have become their family. Affiliate marketing goes beyond just advertising. You can become a member of a brand, you can become a part of the family and have a really awesome experience being an affiliate marketer. Reading this chapter will not only equip you with the right knowledge of choosing the right affiliate program, but it also gives you an insight into why you should partner with a great brand. You get to secure your bag while enjoying what you do at the same time. It's a win-win!

. . .

How do you choose the right affiliate program? Well, let's get started!

Be what you represent: Have you heard of the term "Mirror your passion"? Well, you have probably never heard of it, because I think I just made it up. The point here cannot be stressed enough, the point is to make your business reflect who you are, ensure you are selling your passion and you would never work all your life. People say when you do what you love, it's basically not considered a job because it's leisure all through. As cliché as this sounds, it's true to an extent. It's very true because people get easily worn out when they aren't doing what they love doing. At the same time, it isn't entirely true because no job is actually easy. Even when you are doing what you love, you still need to put in energy and great work and that could be sometimes exhausting although the entire process sometimes feels like fun and the end product brings you fulfilment. For instance, I'm a writer who enjoys writing and I'm really passionate about my job but it doesn't mean I do not feel tired sometimes. However, I would choose writing over any other thing out there because it is passion and it brings me fulfilment. The point here is to ensure you love the brand you are affiliating with, well not actually affiliating (coming together with the company). But, if you want to choose an affiliate program, you should consider yourself being a part of the brand's family and if you want to have a good experience being in the family, you must choose a brand you love and are passionate about. Select products you trust but do not restrict yourself to only the products you are familiar with, give yourself a chance to trust other products too by doing proper research and ensuring that the products are recommendable to your audience. Get familiar with the products even if you do not really feel passionate about the product.

. . .

What are your competitors doing: Another great way to choose an affiliate program especially if you already have an affiliate program, is to check you're your competitors are doing? If a lot of your competitors are choosing a particular affiliate program, you may want to see if there's something attractive about such a program. You can also check if your brand's competitors have a program you can join, remember this is strictly work and there's no such thing as LOYALTY, you can partner with as many brands as you want, you are the one who gets to decide which one you want to join. There's nothing wrong with making other similar products available to your audience. In order to do this, you can research to see if there are similar products to the ones you are already working with.

You can go with what your target audience love: Another amazing way to choose an affiliate program is to genuinely ask to know what your audience would love. Whatever product you decide to promote must be something that resonates with your target audience. Do proper research to ensure you are on the same page with your audience. Do not just assume that they love a particular thing without checking to see if you are accurate. You can use google analytics to see who is buying your product and you can easily get to know what their preferences are, by using such a method. You can also do this by asking your audience directly; using email and other methods to know what they like. Sometimes, you never know what they like unless you ask them directly. You can also go online to see what your target audience is always looking for and the ki9nd of solutions they are always looking for. This is a way to get into the mind of your audience to find out what they like and what their interests would be. Once you can find a program that clearly solves the problem of your audience, you can rest assured that you are on the right path already.

. . .

You should consider Commission levels and earnings per click: One other way to know what type of affiliate program to choose is to carefully examine the commission rates and earning per click. Various affiliate programs offer different commission rates and it is a wise thing to examine the commission levels before you consider an affiliate program. While it seems wise to concentrate on the commission level, it is wiser to pay attention to the bigger picture. Most people fail to do this as they think that higher commissions are everything. Only those who are professionals in the field have enough knowledge to understand that some brands offer higher commissions when they have very low sales while other brands with lower commission rates may sell out really fast. It's really not the same thing, you have to be careful when making your decision. There's a need to understand this on a conceptual level.

The point here is that you will earn more from a program offering a lower commission rate with high sales than the other way round.

You should consider products selling at a higher rate: People often think that expensive products are harder to promote. Your major focus should be on a product that promises to solve the problems of your audience as long as it solves the problems of your audience, the price shouldn't really matter. As long as you trust the brand, have faith in it and you can convince your audience to purchase such products, you will make more money and be fine. While it is reasonable to sell both cheap and expensive products as an affiliate marketer in order to cut across to several people out there, regardless of their social class, it is still advisable to sell both higher rate products and lower-rate ones. Sometimes, vendors may pay you extra money if your customer comes back to purchase the product. While this shouldn't be your focus, the bonus comes off as extra money.

You should consider Upsells: Upsells are a great way to make more money as an affiliate marketer. After a customer buys a particular product, such customer is offered a list of several available products at the same time of purchase which is a process known as "Upselling". This is an added advantage for the affiliate marketer as he gets an extra commission if this happens. For example, a customer may buy a mobile phone using your affiliate link, this person may be offered a special deal that offers a pouch and extra charge. If this customer takes this offer, it means you get paid an additional commission.

Consider the quality of the product: When choosing an affiliate program, it is in the best interest of your audience to ensure the product is of great quality. One of the best ways to ensure your customers are happy is to ensure you are recommending a quality product. You have to ensure you keep your reputation intact when promoting any product. You have to ensure that your audience would never lose their trust in you as it is necessary to maintain a long term relationship.

Consider the Vendor's backing: Affiliate marketing experience can be thrilling. It all depends on who your vendor is. Your vendor can support you in several ways to make you affiliate experience a beautiful one. Email support, live chat and all those can go a long way in helping you learn and can also help you ensure that you deliver your best services as a marketer. A noteworthy vendor makes all the difference. Some companies are always very ready to assist you, they provide you with literally all you need and ensure you have all the necessary material for promoting their brand. You must ensure you put all these to good use and you can come up with creative methods to make these things work in your favour.

Consider the status and reputation of the company: While it is true that there are several developing companies out there, there is an avenue for growth and everyone starts their journey from somewhere, it is very crucial to pay attention to companies who have already built their reputation to an extent. Set your own standards and ensure that the company you want to choose a program from, ticks all your boxes correctly. Although you do not have to wave off new vendors or upcoming companies if they tend to pay well and they seem to have great standards, you can take a risk on them. Never the less, it is important to earn when choosing an affiliate program, however, you can earn more from doing something you are really passionate about.

SUMMARY

You must go for affiliate programs that complement your website. For instance, if your niche has to do with "fashion", go for affiliate programs in the same niche as "fashion dresses, shoes, etc. Do not go for a program that's outside your own niche. It is a bad idea to choose an affiliate program that has to do with Agriculture when your niche is fashion related.

Secondly, do not go for affiliate programs offering little money. Consider affiliate programs with great commission rates. Since we have various affiliate programs out there with different rates, it's wise to do your research properly and go for the ones that offer high commission. It may take some time to find one that offers a really high commission but you would be surprised to know that there are tons of companies out there that can offer gigantic commission rates. You can also go for two-tier affiliate products. Do not forget that the level of sales a company makes should also determine if you would be choosing such a program.

You should also try to see what your competitors are doing as well as what the competitors of your brand are doing. You can choose to work with different brands with a similar niche. You should also join affiliate programs that can support you in making your experience a great one. Do not forget to check out the quality of a product before choosing such a program. You should also go for companies who have built their reputation over the years.

CHAPTER SEVEN: HOW TO CHOOSE A PROFITABLE AFFILIATE MARKETING NICHE

Most times, when people talk about affiliate marketing, what comes to the mind of so many people is "a very simple way to earn passive income". I know a lot of people who think affiliate marketing basically has to do with sleeping on your couch while your money makes itself. It's the dream of every marketer to let your money work for you even while you are sleeping-just like Bill gates. However, not everyone knows that to earn the "billionaire status" isn't something that happens overnight. The reason so many individuals are going into affiliate marketing business is to earn huge money in a twinkle of an eye. Isn't it such an incredible idea? To sleep and have your money make itself with little or no stress! All you have to do is get an affiliate link and ensure that you convince your audience to make purchases. Before you know it! You already have a great passive income. However, it isn't as easy as people try to make it look. Affiliate marketing doesn't just make you an overnight billionaire. The profit doesn't pour in like magic and it isn't in any way a get-rich scheme. While the industry of affiliate marketing, makes a notable revenue every year, you must know that only very few people are responsible for making a huge profit from affiliate marketing, despite the fact that there are so many people in the industry. While the competition is real in affiliate marketing, only those who try to be at the top of their game make a real deal from affiliate marketing. If you want to earn a living as an affiliate marketer, you must be ready to put in the real work and must be ready to have an edge over your other competitors in the industry.

Do you want to be among the select few who are earning a great deal from affiliate marketing? You must ensure you choose a profitable niche in the affiliate industry to be really successful. I have explored a few of these profitable affiliate niches and I will like to share some of them with you as well as how to choose a profitable niche in the affiliate marketing industry. You already know what affiliate, marketing is and how it works. Affiliate marketing has to do with earning a commission by promoting or advertising other people's businesses and products.

How does affiliate marketing work? It basically involves a company who puts their product on a platform like an amazon, Amazon is desperate to make sure these products are sold, this is why amazon brings these products to the grassroots, giving you and I a chance to come in, sell the products while making some money doing so. They allow us to advertise and showcase these products on our websites in order to make sales. What do you get in return for selling these products? You get paid some money otherwise known as commission.

Affiliate marketing affords you an opportunity to make money in every way depending on the goods you are selling and the kind of traffic you can drive. You make more sales; you make more money. When you drive more traffic, you make more money. You as an affiliate promote an industry's product in an attempt to reach lots of people and make money from doing so. Using this method, so many people out there have made tons of dollars by posting on their popular websites that traffic. There are various magazines, websites and websites that use their platform as an avenue to make money from promoting other people's products. These people are known as affiliate marketers and most times they ensure the affiliate marketing tool goes hand-in-hand with their platform.

There are lots of popular magazines who specialize in using fashion blog posts to promote outfits and affiliate merchandises for sites like Amazon and others. You must have seen such websites and blogs who specialize in doing this. Every merchandise they post on their blog has an affiliate link where you can click and make money as an affiliate marketer.

Such people even go as far as creating or making other alternatives available to you; They simply make sure they upload pictures and products of similar brands so that their audience can choose from any of the available outfits. What this means, is that the affiliate marketer even gets more money from promoting more than one brand or one company's product.

Aside from incorporating affiliate marketing in your website or blog, there are several people out there who have made affiliate marketing the basis of their income. You will be surprised to know that there are lots of websites out there only dedicated to promoting affiliate products.

The entire idea of affiliate marketing is incomplete without the presence of the final consumer. They simply keep the business going and ensure that affiliate marketing is driven for the purpose of making money. The consumer is an important figure in affiliate marketing, without the consumer to purchase your affiliate products, you will make no commission. When there's no commission, it means you make no money. It is crucial to be transparent in your business and affiliate marketing isn't excluded, you can include a disclaimer to let your audience know that you are using affiliate links.

Now that you already know how affiliate marketing really works, let's explore all there is in finding the right affiliate niche.

You need to brainstorm and do your research: This is one thing a lot of people especially marketers tend to run away from. The act of brainstorming and doing research in finding the perfect niche. However, you need to know that finding the right niche is the foundation of your job as an affiliate marketer.

I have personally heard the phrase "find your niche" more than a million times in this lifetime, I'm sure you have probably heard it more often than that. What exactly does it mean to find your Niche? What exactly is a niche? Why is it often mentioned? Is it really important and how does it affect your business as an affiliate marketer? Where do people go to find their niche? And how do you find your niche? Well, let's get started. A niche can be defined as a highly specialized market; it has to do with narrowing your business down to a particular sector. For instance, we have the fashion industry but when picking a niche in the fashion industry, you may decide to go into "Women's hats". Women's clothing is mass-produced and purchased in really large volumes. However, the market for women's hats is produced in a smaller market. Companies producing hats aren't as many and the people buying are not really many. What's the point here? The point is that the niche for women's hats is a niche that's really easy to compete in unlike competing against a fashion clothing line that's really huge. If you want to brainstorm, you need to do your research properly and take note of every little thing you find. Take note of markets that aren't really competitive, a market that isn't really competitive can be easily dominated compared to others. You can also head over to a popular website known as "audience insight", just like the name implies, you get an insight into what your audience wants and what appeals to a smaller audience. You click the explore button which can be found in the right corner, the next thing to do is to click on "the top 100" button and you will be given a list of the top 100 websites on the net at a particular time. Do not get me wrong, this is not to advise you to copy what these sites are doing or imitate their industry. That would be really unnecessary as these sites are the most prominent on the internet at the moment. What do you have to do? All you need do is scroll to the next page or the third page in order to take note of the inclinations and niches in the industries you see. For instance, you may notice that Travel is one of the trendy niches but since it's too broad for an affiliate market niche, the next thing you do is to go to QUORA and put the broad category on Quora. You probably know what Quora is already, it's a website where people get to ask questions about anything at all, it isn't restricted to any topic. You can post anything you have in mind and have millions of people provide an answer to your question. You do not just get an answer, you get a very detailed answer that explains what you want in clear terms and the easiest to understood manner. The next thing you have to do after getting to Quora is to simply search for that broad term like "Travel" in the search bar. You will get a whole list of questions that have been asked in that field or category. The point is to ensure that you get different smaller niches within that broad industry or category. If you do not seem to find something really impressive, you can always go back to Quant cast to find another category.

Check the monetization of this category on Click bank: The next thing you want to do after settling with a particular niche topic is to check the worth of this niche. It is a really futile effort to get into the affiliate marketing industry without knowing the worth of your niche topic. If you can't drive traffic and sales with a niche topic, it's totally pointless. While there are several affiliate networks out there, click bank is an amazing site to start because of the large number of people who use the platform on a daily basis.

In order to get started with checking the worth of your newly-found niche, you can click on the affiliate marketplace option in the top menu. You can commence by searching for your category on the search bar at the top. This is a great way to help you narrow down your niche. However, you have to ensure you check the left-side menu as well as there are already enough topic lists. All you have to do nest is select your category or search for your new-found niche in the search bar and examine your results. Don't be confused, you may not really understand how this process works if you have never used Click Bank before. Why not let's explain it more. Basically, the left side of the menu is where you can literally get search results while the right side has all the result for any topic at all. This is crucial because you can get products you could sell for your niche. It is recommended to get your sorting done by using "Gravity". This metric lets you know how well affiliate product sells within your specified niche. You must carefully examine this search results to know which products seem like they will be easy to sell. You can easily find products with a very high gravity score and products that can help you make lots of money as well. You may not find a product you really want immediately, you need to keep checking until you find something you really want and something you are pleased with. Make sure you settle with a product that's really easy to sell.

Confirm your niche on AdWords: If you want to find a perfect affiliate marketing niche, your search is incomplete without Google AdWords. You get to know the original cost per click of the keywords in your chosen niche. You have to ensure your focus is on driving traffic and meaningful sales, this is why you must know how the competition is in your chosen niche. This is the perfect way to know how you can be at the top of your game. In order to commence, go to Google AdWords' keyword planner. This is where you get to click on the first option in order to find keywords based on category or phrase. The next thing you want to do is put in your niche keywords and pay attention to certain words that would bring you an array of results. You can get great ideas from the diverse lists of related keywords. You can get a perfect idea of what the competition in your niche looks like as well as what the monthly searches are and the suggested bids. You can get an idea of the traffic your niche keyword drives by checking the monthly searches. You can also get to know how difficult it is to rank for your specified keywords. You can also conclude if you would be spending your time on a particular niche by checking the suggested bid. This is a great way to know what marketers are willing to pay for a single click. You can settle for affiliate niches that promise to pay a lot per click. You can go back to click bank in order to search again to narrow your search more. When everything is already in place, it means you have found yourself a lucrative affiliate niche.

Begin to Trade your Merchandise: After finding and settling for a profitable affiliate niche, you are on the verge of making it really big in the affiliate marketing industry. This is when you begin to trade. Your affiliate marketing is incomplete if you do not have the right knowledge to drive great sales. Just like every typical business, if you do not sell, you don't make money. I personally believe that Amazon and click banks are the best affiliate networks and they are my favourite of all. There is no doubt in the fact that Amazon is really effective for e-trading businesses. It is a huge platform for trading online. If you want to sell to a great number of people, Amazon is the right place to go. Joining amazon is absolutely free and it is one of the simplest ways to commence your journey as an affiliate marketer. You can always choose from the array of goods to sell which means you have unlimited offers to choose from or select from. You can also rest assured that there are amazing commissions on Amazon. If you do not find what you want on Amazon (which is almost impossible), you can always try Click bank.

This is the total rundown of all you need to know when it comes to selecting a wonderful affiliate niche. You already know where to look for these products and you can sign up on any of these platforms anytime you want. You can start selling these products on your website or blog.

SUMMARY

While the idea of affiliate marketing seems to be an easy one and the idea of making real

Passive income from affiliate marketing seems like a piece of cake, it isn't as easy as you think it is. You don't just wake up one morning to billions of dollars in your bank account. It doesn't work that way and it isn't that easy at all. In order to make a great passive income from affiliate marketing, you must be really active and be involved in what you are doing. You can activate your affiliate marketing skill by coming up with an effective affiliate niche which allows you to make so much money when done in the proper way. The affiliate marketing industry is a really competitive industry where you get to make real money by getting an edge over every other person in the industry.

In order to settle with a revenue-boosting niche, you must start by making pa roper research and brainstorming just the right way. You start by thinking of a niche that isn't really crowded. You can narrow down your list by making use of quora to check out trendy and really active markets. You can see how much you can get from an affiliate niche by making use of Click bank. Do your further research on Google AdWords' to research your keywords in your new niche. You can also explore diverse areas using the available metrics on google AdWords. After finding the perfect product, start selling your product through Amazon and Click bank. Keep developing your affiliate niche in order to make it real big in the industry. Never forget to grow your traffic.

CHAPTER EIGHT: HOW TO BUILD TRUST AS AN AFFILIATE MARKETER

One thing every affiliate marketer should know is that it is really important for you to build trust in your career. Have you ever been told that most companies and brands only use affiliate marketers because they know that affiliate marketers have a community of people who trust them and believe in their recommendations? Well, now you know why affiliate marketing is always chosen over the traditional way of marketing. Every individual, influencer and marketer out there who has a great following and a community of people who believe in them, actually worked really hard to build that trust. It isn't something that comes to you overnight, you work really hard to get there and while you may have to work your ass off to get a lot of people to trust you, losing the trust base you already have is something that can happen to you at any time. It is easier to lose trust than it is to build trust.

How can you lose the trust you already have? You can stop people from trusting you by recommending products you aren't really sure of. There are certain products that can be detrimental to the health of your audience while there are some that would not solve the problems of your audience. These are products that can shatter the trust base you already have. No matter what sort of business you are into, gaining the trust of people doesn't come easily, it takes a lot of time and could even take years sometimes. There's a saying that says that being in the faces of people for a long time makes people trust you. While this saying isn't properly structured, it is true that when you have been relevant and consistent in whatever you are doing for a long time, people would begin to pay you the attention and would also begin to listen to you. Sometimes, the temptation to make money at the expense of losing your trust could be overwhelming but you must refuse to be tempted as this may cost you more than you can imagine. Affiliate marketing is a business that requires the trust of your audience to thrive because it involves selling and you can't sell to your audience if they don't trust you. You need to earn their trust and you shouldn't be tempted to do anything that could result in losing the trust of your audience, regardless of how much money is at stake.

I have personally encountered several situations where I was tempted to promote products I wasn't really sure of; I was being offered a tremendous amount of money but I knew what was at stake here! The trust of my readers has always been important to me and I would never compromise it for anything in the world. You would be surprised to realize how much an immense community that trust you, could give you. You would be overjoyed if you knew how special you could be to an audience who have great trust in you. It actually gladdens my heart to know that there are people out there who are confident in the fact that they can count on my words. I tell you, there's no greater feeling to hear someone say "If you are recommending it, then it really has to be good". There's a wonderful feeling that comes with knowing that so many people trust you enough to listen to you, especially if these people are people who have never met you before. They are across the globe and they probably don't even have an idea of what you look like in person, yet they trust you immensely! They trust you enough to listen to your advice, your recommendations and even go far beyond that, they tell other people about you and refer their family and friends to you. There's no better feeling than this. I personally know a few affiliate marketers who have been tempted to recommend or promote the wrong products for money. Those who couldn't resist temptation had to pay dearly for it. Although there are others who could get lucky and may not get caught, however, it doesn't take long before something happens to their career and they lose a great deal. You may not believe in Karma but in Affiliate marketing, there's no escaping it. You may be tempted to even keep promoting a wrong brand because you make decent money from doing so, however, the wisest thing to do is to ensure you disassociate yourself from such brand. Your reputation as a brand or a website should come first before any other thing. If it's going to dent your image, it's definitely not worth giving a try.

You may lose some money from dissociating yourself from a brand or website or even lose your ranking but if it's to keep the trust of your audience, it's worth it.

One major way to succeed with any online business is knowing and understanding the formula and having the right knowledge to thrive. You already know that affiliate marketing is one of the numerous legitimate ways to make money online. While it is a great way to make money, there are certain challenges that come with it, just like any other legitimate business. In order to help you have an edge over the numerous people in the industry of affiliate marketing, several guides have been designed and put in place to assist you in your journey. However, the problem is that majority of these so-called guides aren't really detailed and they tell you only the basics you need to know, they hardly delve into the real and undiluted truth about affiliate marketing. While a lot of these guides would only tell about how to generate leads and how to drive traffic and other basic things like conversion and others. They barely ever tell you about personal relationships. Personal relationships should be built and maintained in every business especially one like affiliate marketing that involves selling to lots of people you have never met before on the internet.

Why should you build personal relationships and is it really important to build personal relationships?

I want you to know that it is really crucial to building relationships. You must understand why relationships are an integral part of affiliate marketing and online businesses in general. The basic truth and foundational fact are that most people would rather patronize someone they are familiar with. It's like having a friend who sells pets and then meeting a random person who introduces himself as someone who sells pets. Who would you rather patronize? Only one out of ten people would patronize the random person at the expense of his friend. What's the point here? Personal relationship! If they are very familiar with you, they would even go as far as referring someone to you. When you build genuine and healthy relationships with people, you can actually increase your direct sales and these people can trust you with their problems when they believe in you. They tell you their problems and would never take your proffered solutions for granted. Trust in affiliate marketing goes as far as having your audience discuss their future and ask you important questions. The major idea here is that building trust in affiliate marketing will help your business go very far.

HOW DO YOU BUILD A SOLID RELATIONSHIP AS AN AFFILIATE MARKETER?

Building a solid relationship as an affiliate marketer is something that requires certain steps.

Know yourself: If you want to build a strong relationship as an affiliate, the very first step is to know who you are. Know your motivation and what actually drives you as well as what you are willing to offer other people. You must examine some really crucial things, to begin with, ask yourself what you want from your business, know why you are passionate about a particular company as well as your affiliate products. Know what your passion is and listen to what your heart says in order to know what kind of goals you have for your business. If you do not know yourself and if you are not at peace with who you are, it would be difficult to develop any bond with other people. You must first ensure that you are in good sync with who you are in order to build a relationship with other people. You may be wondering what finding yourself has to do with building a relationship with others, but it is more important than you think. This is because you cannot give what you do not have. Being in sync with yourself is a great way to connect with others and it can have a realty amazing effect on your business.

Be curious and be ready to help: This is another great way to build a relationship with people. You need to become a problem solver to build a relationship with people. If you become passionate about finding what bugs the heart of each individual you encounter while proffering good solutions, you will be surprised to know that it would really help you in your career as an affiliate marketer. For example, imagine meeting someone who has difficulty losing weight; someone who is struggling with YO-YO dieting, this person keeps struggling with keeping to certain diet restrictions. You may have a product that would help restrict their meals. This is one way to proffer solutions to people's problems.

Imagine knowing an individual who's been trying to do an online job but he lost the motivation to do that. You could offer a solution by selling them an EBook that helps them find motivation again and helps them decide to work from home. The need to always be honest in your approach can never be over-emphasized. You can try by asking questions in order to know how you can come in and how you can help them solve their problems. This is one effective way to build mutually-beneficial relationships.

Build Digital Relationships: While there is a popular belief that Social media helps people connect and also helps to build relationships, the real truth is that social media has made it really difficult for us to connect and has also made the building of relationships more difficult. Most people just assume that spamming other people constantly is a way to build a relationship. This is a very wrong way to approach this and spamming others irritates them and makes them really angry. If you have already started your journey as an affiliate, you should really reflect on how you use your social media profiles. Do you just post your affiliate links on your profile? Well, there's actually nothing wrong with that, but you should be using your social media profiles for something much better. You should build reasonable relationships with your profile. There's nothing wrong with getting personal with your audience to a certain level. Let them in on what your personal life looks like and make them feel like they actually know you. You should also let them know how your products have personally helped you in your affairs. Build a relationship by asking them questions and urging them to answer your questions in a way to strike meaningful conversations. You should also discuss with them and always be ready to develop a good relationship that can help you convert your relationship with them into leads. The point is to ensure you use your digital access to build reasonable relationships, other than generating leads and driving sales. It won't hurt you to get personal to a certain level. It will definitely go a long way in influencing your sales positively.

Never forget the art of following up: One crucial thing you also need to pay attention to is the art of follow up. Do not just stop at building relationships alone, it is super necessary to follow up with people. We live in an era where people do not think there's anything wrong in ghosting on others. They simply relate with you well right now and then stop responding or completely forget about you. This isn't a nice thing to do if you are seeking to build a solid relationship as an affiliate marketer. Ghosting on people only makes them worry about what they must have done wrong. You leave them completely clueless and they have no idea why you stopped texting them. This is one way to ruin even the best kinds of relationships. You need to keep following up to know what they are passionate about, know their interests. If they patronized you, you should know what they felt about such a product and how it helped them solve certain problems. These reviews would help you know where your business stands as well as what needs to be put in place. Follow up with your audience to keep them updated about all you are doing, this shows them that they are special to you in a way and they are more than just a number to you. It is a great way to establish strong relationships with people. Trust is the foundation of every relationship out there, it isn't just limited to romantic relationships alone. Without trust in a relationship, it crumbles at the slightest glitch and such a relationship would never stand the test of time. It is really important that people can actually count on your words and take your words for it. I keep stressing the fact that there is an awesome feeling that comes with knowing how much trust people have in you and knowing that they would follow your recommendations without questioning your credibility. You also need to start trusting other people if you expect the same gesture from people. Trusting people comes with a certain degree of peace of mind, you know you don't have to worry because you have faith in certain people and y0u know they would only do what's in your best interest. It means you can leave certain things in the hands of people without stressing or bothering about such things. When you may be very concerned about building trust, you need to also evaluate what certain people think about you and your attitude, especially when it comes to your credibility.

There are several benefits of building trust and building a community of people who have great and immense trust in you. You are able to defend yourself and stand up for yourself without getting on the nerves of anyone. It teaches you how to become a really assertive individual. Although, we cannot help having issues with others in our day-day activities and you must also be ready to come to terms with the fact that not everyone will like you, regardless of how hard you try or how good you think you are. Some people will still find a fault in your personality, no matter how well you treat them. They just never seem to be pleased with whatever you do! They are the people who say things like "*I don't just like that Guy or I don't even like that girl, she irritates me and I don't know why*" Such people have a chronic problem and it's not your fault that they don't like you. It's completely fine to not be liked by everyone. You don't have to force it, it's something that comes naturally.

Here's a list of other ways to build trust in order to achieve real success in every area of your life including your personal life and career life:

ALWAYS MAKE PROMISES YOU CAN KEEP: You must know that building trust means having people believe you, stand up for you and root for you even in your absence. In order to do this, you should never make any promise you cannot keep. If you promise to do something for them or promise to be there for some people at a particular time, you need to keep to your word and do just that. When they hand you over a task, you should make them feel rest assured that they can forget about it completely because you will not fail them in any way. There will be times you will regret making certain promises but because you value your relationship with such a person, you decide to through with the promise regardless. You would only learn to be more careful in future in order to avoid making a commitment you will later regret. If you ever have to turn your back on a promise, it is only necessary to make this known beforehand so you do not break the heart of the person too much. The only reason so many people end up breaking their promises is that they have a problem of not knowing how to say no. Saying Yes to people even when it isn't convenient for you isn't a way of building trust, it is nothing but total cowardice. Because you are scared of saying No and you are scared of hurting that person, you agree to things you will later regret. You really need to learn how to say No sometimes, because you end up ruining things if you fail to turn down certain offers. You may fail to meet up with a certain deadline or fail to deliver a quality service if you let the fear of saying No overwhelm you. These outcomes are really disastrous as they leave you with creating an impression of someone who isn't credible in any way. You would avoid such a scenario by learning to say No at certain times. This means you should learn the importance of keeping your promises. As an affiliate marketer, you should remember to keep to your promises when recommending certain products. One other advantage of keeping to your word is the fact that people would most likely treat you the same way you treat others, and you may notice that people would start keeping to their words when dealing with you.

Start Living your own values: This is really important in building a strong relationship with people. You need to have certain values and stick to these values when dealing with people. Treat people the same way you want to be treated; if you desire trust from people, learn to trust people. If you are seeking to build friendship, show people want it means to be nice and what true friendship means. 2. Learn how to communicate effectively with others

Learn how to be consistent: Sometimes, we cannot help but wonder why there are so many relationships falling apart in our environment. Today, you are absolutely on the same page with someone and everything goes well in your connection with that person, the next minute, you guys aren't even talking anymore. Most relationships fall apart because people don't know the true value of communication. People have bad communication skills and they keep wondering why relationships aren't working out. Just to be clear here, I'm talking about all kinds of relationships here including business relationships. Make sure people get your points clearly and understand exactly where you are coming from. Ensure your ideas are passed in such a way that your audience can clearly understand what your point is and where you are driving at. When dealing with money, you shouldn't assume things. You should never get tired of clarifying things and repetition is important when needed. Do the meaning of trust, it isn't when you fail to discuss sensitive issues with an assumption that the other person understands, trust is when you decide to discuss the sensitive issues and ensure that the other individual knows exactly why you are having such a conversation.

Building trust isn't totally free of risk. It isn't something that just happens by chance. Trust happens when you have given other people a chance to prove that they are worthy and it is also the act of taking every chance you get, to show people that they can count on you. Solid communication makes all the difference and ensuring that you are on the same page with your audience is always a very wise thing to do. You should talk so that other people can listen to you.

Know that it is something that comes with time: You do not just meet someone in one day and begin to trust them. It is something that actually comes with time, it is a gradual process and it doesn't happen in one day. You shouldn't expect people to trust you just like that, understand that you have to put in certain efforts if they have to trust you. Know that they must be convinced that you are trustworthy before they trust you. Trust is like investing, the only difference with investing money is that people are investing g emotions by trusting you. They need to be 100 % sure that they are safe before giving themselves a chance to trust you. As soon as people get comfortable with you, they can begin to invest their trust in you. When something goes wrong in every kind of relationship including business, most people are very quick to pass the blame onto other people. People don't feel like they are responsible for every glitch that happens in a relationship as much as the other person as well. You must be responsible if you want to build trust with people.

If you want to build trust with people, show them that they can trust you and take some chances on them too. Trust them and you will be trusted in return. Building trust as an affiliate, the marketer should be viewed this way, would you propose marriage after meeting someone who ticks all your boxes correctly on a first date? The answer is No. Regardless of how amazing you think this person is, you would definitely want to give yourself some time to know this person to an extent before taking a risk like marriage with some stranger. This only happens in a Disney fairy tale movie; it isn't something that happens every time in real life. This is exactly the way it is with building trust as an affiliate marketer. You need to give yourself time and take things one step at a time, failure to do this by expecting too much immediately only means you will scare people away.

Do not make rash decisions: Most times, people disagree because they fail to weigh their decisions properly before making such decisions. You don't have to be that person who agrees to do something they didn't want to do. Before you commit to anything, ensure that you have weighed the pros and cons of your decision effectively before jumping into conclusions. Do not bite more than you can chew and never take on more things than you can handle so you do not come off as an unserious person or someone who isn't trustworthy. Do not say Yes when you already have so much on your plate. When you agree to deadlines that aren't reasonable or you decide to go beyond your own strength, you will most likely regret it. Another thing you need to pay attention to is personal organization and discipline, when people see how personally organized and disciplined you are, they find it really easy to trust you. You may be scared of losing certain relationships when you do not agree to take more than you can handle but such people will have to understand that you refuse to be pressured or harassed into doing what you wouldn't do.

Never take the trust of your audience for granted: After building relationships with people for years, we tend to get comfortable with having these people in our lives and we begin to take them for granted. Before realizing that we no longer treat these people with respect, it takes an eternity and forever to know this. You should never get used to having people around, it's important to appreciate the people in your life. No matter how busy you get, find time to reach out to the people you have built a relationship with. Even in normal relationships, seeing people regularly can stop you from valuing them and respecting them. You begin to think you don't need to make any effort but there's great need to make some efforts. It makes people feel special and valued. We don't realize how our loved ones go an extra mile to ensure we are good and to ensure our relationship is secured until something happens and this person no longer does what they used to do. We shouldn't wait until we lose those who are important to us before realizing how much they mean to us and we should never get tired of showing people that we truly care.

Consistency is a great way to build a relationship and we should not fail to acknowledge those who are always there for us. These people are always people who have earned our trust over the years. No matter what kind of bridge that stands between you and such people, this bridge should be crossed as we need to show these people how much we care. While you may not always be there for the people who trust you, you must show them that you can be available for them by maintaining regular communication with such people and ensuring that you stay connected. We should show the people in our lives that there is always a place for them in our lives.

Appreciate your customers for doing business with you: The power of appreciation goes a long way in maintaining relationships. Most people do not see gratitude as a virtue but it is worth paying great attention to. You may get carried away with building trust with new people and creating new relationships, at the expense of making sure your previous relationships are properly nurtured. You must learn to maintain existing relationships by appreciating these people for taking a chance on you. It is a very crucial thing that some people forget to execute. Throwing away old relationships because you want to form new ones is a mistake you would definitely regret making. Most times, you never reconnect with these people ever again. I know a particular who wanted to do business with a very wealthy personality; the thought of it seemed impossible and just as expected, this wealthy personality refused to do business when he was approached. However, this Businessman never gave up, he kept on making calls and when he remained consistent in his approach, this wealthy personality changed his mind and decided to take a chance on this businessman. What does this preach? It preaches nothing but consistency, showing up consistently can be really effective for building trust. When you give up immediately, you risk the chance of driving certain sales. You have to keep on trying because it is a better option to try instead of imagining what would have happened if you had tried. You must also know that the best-sellers aren't the people who are only concerned with making sales. They are the people who are genuinely interested in solving their client's problems. When you are driven by the motivation to solve problems instead of making sales, your audience and customer can see through you and read your intentions. This is a great way to win them over to your side. When a customer doesn't need to purchase a product right now and you keep persisting, they would most likely remember you when they are ready to purchase such products. It actually requires putting in a certain degree of efforts and it also requires patience on your side. However, your efforts will definitely pay off when these customers finally decide to patronize you by clicking on your affiliate link to make certain purchases. Only the consistent seller or marketer has an edge over everyone else in the affiliate marketing industry. Learning how to genuinely appreciate your customers and being consistent in your dealings is a great way to build trust.

Constantly develop your team skills: When you find yourself in any team, it is important to build trust in order to enhance cooperation and a spirit of teamwork. You will never achieve success as a team if you do not take out time to build trust and maintain your relationship. You have a responsibility to your team and you will be very wrong to be that one person who hardly ever contributes anything in a team. If you happen to be that person who isn't expressive or who seems not have any opinion, it would be really difficult to earn the trust of your teammates. However, if you choose to be a responsible team member who contributes greatly and a person who is always ready to discuss issues especially really essential topics, it means you have proven to your team members that they can actually trust you. How does this concern an affiliate marketer? Being ready and available to discuss with your audience is a great way to build trust with your audience. You should be ready to embrace the ideas of your audience, show them that you believe their ideas are really important to you. If you feel that someone has offered brilliant advice or opinion, you shouldn't hesitate to tell them that you value their opinion and you should tell them how brilliant you think their idea is. Feeling that you respect their ideas is a great way to build a relationship with people. Be genuinely interested in your audience's complaints and let them know how you feel about their grievances. These are ways to show how much you really care about them and how you value them as your customers. It is normal to not always agree with what people would say but even when you do not buy the idea of your audience, the best way to deal with it is to not directly counter their opinions, let them know why you do not think their idea is a great one in the best way possible. Make sure your feedback is a constructive one that demonstrates and presents your ideas in the most respectful way. Always show that you are actively involved when attending to your audience.

Cultivate an attitude of being honest: The phrase "Honesty is the best policy" isn't a cliché at all, it is a fact that should always be remembered. You need to always be honest to yourself and everyone around you. Being honest is indeed an amazing way of building trust. Most people tend to tell "little lies" or white lies because they want to avoid getting into trouble or because they don't want to appear imperfect. What people fail to remember is the fact that relationships can easily be destroyed when you fail to say the truth and the other person gets to know that you haven't really been honest with them. This is one of the numerous ways to lose people's trust in you- Telling lies. No matter how small you think a lie is or how "white" you think it is, a lie is a lie and it can go a long way in tainting your image and ruining your reputation. You may think the lie is so little but you may realize how big the consequence of a small lie can actually be. No matter how well you want to sound and how beautiful you want your story to be, never tell lies in the name of "embellishing the truth". Always call a spade a spade if you want your audience to trust you. If you ever get caught telling a lie, you must keep in mind that people will always interpret a story in their minds no matter how you present it. Am I digressing? No, I'm only trying to say that people would trust you less if they found out that you haven't really been truthful to them. This would definitely influence the way people interpret your actions and the things you say. If they think you are not saying the truth, they would interpret in a negative way whatever you say or do to them. Just a single lie can affect the impression people have about you. If you think telling a lie would be a great way to protect people, it means you do not trust them enough to deal with certain things and it is still a way to destroy the trust of people in you.

Always be willing to render assistance to people: If you really want to build trust in your relationship with your audience, you must be ready to be of help to people when they need your help. When you show people how much you care about them by helping them when you have nothing to gain in return, you will find out that you will win the hearts of people and also earn their trust. Very little acts of kindness can go a long way in building a trust-worthy relationship. You do not have to render helps that would hurt you in certain ways, don't do things when it's going to affect you. You shouldn't help others at the expense of meeting your own important deadlines or events. The fact that you are kind to people doesn't mean you have to take their place in doing their jobs. Helping people identify certain solutions to their problems and offering them a piece of advice can pass as a great act of kindness. Taking responsibility for other people's mistakes isn't in any way an act of kindness. This is not the right way to go about building trust, it means you are-teaching them on how to be overly dependent. They would never learn to take charge of their lives or grow as individuals. You should teach them how to solve their own issues so they do not take you for granted in the name of trusting you. You must ensure that you are genuinely being Kind in your efforts to build trust. Do not foster dependence by trying to be kind even when it isn't convenient.

Always express your feelings: People have always tried to not to show their feelings in order to seem strong and dodge the look of being defenceless. If you want people to trust you, you have to learn how to be real. Show them exactly how you feel and what goes on in your head. People find it easy to trust people when they feel like they have something in common with such people. If you make your audience feel like they can relate with you on a personal level, they begin to to to trust you. Having a fake exterior and pretending to be who you are not is not a way to build trust in relationships. Your audience can tell if or not you are being original and originality is relatable and trustworthy. When they know how honest your emotions are, they begin to feel like they are on the same page with you and begin to develop some trust in you. There are certain people especially celebrities I thought I didn't like, I didn't like them because I had never gotten a chance to know them on a personal level and I never knew really much about them. I recently became a huge fan of one of such people whom I had never given myself a chance to know in my entire life. However, reading the book of this celebrity in question made me get an insight into the person's mind and I began to feel like we had so many things in common. Today, I'm not just an ordinary fan, I'm obsessed. When people get to know that you have feelings just like them and when they get to know that you are honest in your expressions, they begin to take some chances on you.

Take for instance, when you have pent-up anger about a person who probably doesn't even know you are angry with him, you become angry when this person who is oblivious of his sins is going about his life happily. Yet, you do not want to confront them because you want to avoid creating a scene or raising a conflict, you will only end up becoming angrier than before. Instead, choosing to develop a constructive criticism makes you get on the same page with the other person and you both find a way to deal with this issue. Being emotionally intelligent doesn't mean you have to ignore feelings that do not go well with you. Being emotionally intelligent means understanding the way you feel and taking the necessary actions.

Never be selfish: You must ensure you think about other people first. Commend people when there is a need to commend them and show them that you believe in them. Building trust means you do not always be in a haste to take all the credit for a particular thing all the time. When building trust with people, you have to care enough to give them their needed recognition every time they deserve it. This is a great way to build a community of people who are willing to go an extra mile when it comes to helping you. These are the people who would readily listen to your advice and recommendations as well as refer you to others as well. Have you ever rendered help to someone who didn't show any appreciation for the help you rendered? How did you feel? You probably felt unappreciated and you might have even decided not to help such people in future. This is why you shouldn't be selfish in taking all the credit, you should give others their deserved credit as well. It goes a long way in gilding a relationship with people and building trust you as well. If you fail to appreciate people for the help they rendered, it means you are selfish. It doesn't matter if these people were meant to help you, never forget to say thank you because of a feeling of entitlement. You would barely hear people complain about not being properly appreciated but you have to take out of your busy schedule to show them how much you value and appreciate their support. If you happen to be someone who never praises people when they do something good, you have to stop complaining about things you aren't pleased with. Focus on commenting on something good once in a while and praise people when it is important to.

Listen to your instincts: Sometimes we think building trust has to do with listening and doing other people's biddings without complaining. However, you must know that building trust by seeking the trust of others is a terrible way of building relationships with people. You have to constantly sacrifice so much for people if you are always seeking approval. People would take advantage of you this way, instead of trusting you, they trample upon you because they know you are willing to bend over backwards for their sake. On the other hand, listening to your instincts even when others don't agree with you is a great way to get people to respect you and build your reputation the right way. While this may seem out of place, you need to know that you will step on others while you are seeking to build trust with people. If y0ou keep avoiding clashing with people or you always want people to say something good about you, you will never have a standpoint in life. Because you don't want to offend other people, you shut out your idea and opinions because you don't want to step on others. Instead of building trust, you will only find out that a lot of people would regard you as a "coward" for not having a voice. You must have a standpoint in life, it is either you are for something or against something and your opinions and personal beliefs are what help you gain the trust of others.

Admit that you are wrong: One great way to build trust is to admit that you are wrong when you make mistakes. For instance, as an affiliate marketer, if you found out that there was something wrong with an affiliate product of yours, you must apologize and admit your mistakes. This is how to show your audience that you actually care about them. Since your audience also human beings who are far from being perfect, they will most likely forgive you and forget about your mistakes. Sociology shows that you are most likely to trust people who admit their mistakes and people who do not pretend to be who they are not. Accepting who you are, being original and admitting your mistakes are all excellent ways to build trust in relationships.

CHAPTER NINE: THE RIGHT WAY TO USE SOCIAL MEDIA FOR AFFILIATE MARKETING

Learning how to use social media properly can go a long way in helping your business as an affiliate marketer. You must know that so many people have made money from using social media for affiliate marketing. It is one of the most effective and quickest ways to make money online. Since you are an external force helping a company to promote their products, you must know that earning a commission by using social media for Affiliate marketing is something that requires strategic planning and a certain degree of knowledge. Although using social media for affiliate marketing is an amazing way to generate money, you need to ensure that your social media isn't only used for pasting affiliate links but you must ensure that your social media accounts are valuable to your business is a great way.

When you make posts without value, you can make your audience lose interest in the message you are passing which can certainly rub off on your s an affiliate marketer much more than you can imagine. You do not just have to make your social media posts about promotions alone, you can share other interesting things as well in order to get the attention of your audience and keep their interest in your profile.

What are the strategic ways to use social media for affiliate marketing?

There are numerous idea and guides that can be used for earning a great deal from using social media from affiliate marketing. Building a community of people who can relate to your ideas on social media is a great way to enhance your affiliate marketing business. You should consider doing the following to ensure that there is a smooth connection between you and your audience on your social media platforms, to promote and advance your career as an affiliate marketer:

Endeavour to create a redirect link: People can now easily identify affiliate links when they see them. Since so many people are quite familiar with affiliate links, it is advisable to make use of redirect links that look straight forward and simple. A straightforward link is a link that captivates and entices your audience to press the click button.

Pay attention to your content: Whenever you are making use of social media for affiliate marketing, you need to pay great attention to your content. Evaluate what kind of posts you make and ask yourself really thoughtful questions to know what your content looks like. Are your posts able to stand on their own without your affiliate links? Are your posts actually valuable to your audience? Know whether your posts are able to influence your audience in any way or not. Know if your posts are captivating enough and know if they attract the right kind of people. When you use the right method and you have the right knowledge, you can learn how to use your social media platforms to reach out to the right kind of people. You have to ensure that your content is actually there and you have something really unique to give your audience. Ensure that your content is interesting enough to grab the attention of the right people and to reach the right kind of people out there. Try to consider a few contents you really like and ask yourself why you like such contents. Note these things and implement them in your own content as well. Ensure that your content is worthy enough to hold the interest of your audience.

Ensure you make use of pictures: Every picture tells a story. You have probably heard of this saying before. It is true that when you see a picture, you can imagine a few things in your head and a few scenarios in your head. Pictures are really important as they help us in documenting our journey through life and help us keep track of certain things and important events in our lifetime. Using pictures for affiliate marketing on your social media platforms is an amazing way to grab the attention of your audience on your social media platforms. When you see a picture, especially a creative and captivating one when scrolling through your feed, you are probably intrigued and you instantly stop to see these pictures. Incorporating pictures in your affiliate marketing journey, will interest your audience and grab their attention. This is one of the reasons why so many people who are into affiliate marketing decide to use Instagram to promote their journey in affiliate marketing. You get to see how powerful photos are when you see how much affiliate marketers who use Instagram as their affiliate marketing platform actually make on a daily basis. This means pictures are really important in your journey as an affiliate marketer seeking to use social media as an avenue to promote affiliate marketing.

Pay attention to really quality affiliate products: This is a very important thing every affiliate marketer out there needs to keep in mind. You need to link to quality products if you really want to be successful while using social media for affiliate marketing. It doesn't matter how many pictures you use or how attractive your posts look. If you do not link to really quality products, you will find it difficult to earn something from affiliate marketing. If you are rooting for a product you are passionate about, you can impress your audience to want to purchase your affiliate products. You can even make more money by recommending more than a couple of products you are passionate about.

Have an online presence: Another amazing way to use social media for affiliate marketing is to ensure that you have an online presence. Being regular online means you are always available to answer any questions your audience may have. It also means that you are actively involved in what you do by posting regularly and maintaining a regular connection and regular communication with your audience. This is why you shouldn't exhaust yourself by using numerous social media platforms. It wears you off and wears you out. If you really want to maintain a regular online presence, you need to ensure you concentrate on one or two platforms alone. When you become really comfortable communicating and posting on these ones, you can then include other ones. This should only happen when you have ensured that your audience is already well catered for and in good hands. You can maintain an online presence by setting aside a few hours every day to building your affiliate marketing efforts on your social media platforms.

Build a connection with other affiliates: You will be surprised to know that there are tons of people out there who are into affiliate marketing. If you maintain a regular connection with some of them, they can help you learn a few things including how to use social media for affiliate marketing. Just like the word "Social media", socializing is really important if you want to go a long way as an affiliate marketer. You can team up with several other affiliates to share links, give each other a shout out and help each other improve your following while helping you put your affiliate links out there. Do not see other affiliates as your rivals or your enemies, make yourself comfortable with learning from them and cooperating with them. You can really benefit from learning and cooperating with other affiliates. They can help your growth in your journey as an affiliate and help you attain great success. Being ready to listen to other people is a great way to learn from people and emulate their footsteps in becoming successful.

The advent of Social media is one of the most beautiful things that have ever happened to Millennials. It is a great tool for marketing and promoting your business. Social media can be very great for promoting your affiliate marketing and putting your affiliate products out there. Most people don't think it is necessary but it is really essential for your success as an affiliate marketer. All you need to do is to ensure that you follow certain rules and regulations, you also need to master a few tips and strategies. Before you know it, you have already become a successful affiliate marketer who uses social media for affiliate marketing. The idea of social media isn't in any way difficult to comprehend and can be easily understood by someone who's never used it before. The same procedures you use for putting out content is the same you use to promote your affiliate marketing experience. These strategies are strategies that have been used over the years by people who have benefited greatly from affiliate marketing. You can also benefit from the strategies in a great way if you put them to use correctly.

SUMMARY

In this chapter, we talked about great ways to leverage social media for affiliate marketing.

Social media affords lots of affiliate marketers an opportunity to make money by using their platforms to their own advantage. Comprehending every social network's viewers, structures, and messaging proficiencies is critical to make something out of your online presence. Here is a list of important techniques, intuitions and guidelines to relief you and assist you in successfully integrating social media in your affiliate marketing business which we talked about in this chapter.

You need to learn how to keep certain Pitches for Your website: The only way to engage your audience and grab their attention is to ensure they find your page or platform exciting enough to want to stay a little bit longer. Do not only restrict your social channels to promoting your affiliate links alone, but it is also a platform to create some fun and grab the attention of your audience. You should save the strong promotions for your pages and websites. Ensure that your social media platforms are used for entertaining and captivating your audience. Your audience will most likely visit your social platforms for the fun and creative content you are known for putting up. Know your target audience as well as what interests them in order to captivate them and keep them really interested in checking out your content. When they visit your page, ensure that there is something that makes them want to stay and something that makes them want to exhaust all their data on your page. The best way to do this is to ensure that your content is nothing but charming and exquisite. Do not also forget to Create redirect links that make it really easy and straightforward to check out your links.

Make use of captivating Photos and Videos: If you want to use social media for affiliate marketing, one of the effective ways to do so is via the use of pictures and captivating videos. There is something known as the visual power and it is what keeps the interest of people alive after viewing a particular thing. You must use this visual power to your advantage by making use of visually captivating things like videos and pictures. People pay more attention to visually interesting things than text-only ones. You can post pictures that promote your products as well as videos that clearly illustrate how to make use of those products. You can easily find such short captivating videos on Instagram. They are mostly used for promoting affiliate products.

Be actively involved online: There is a great need to have an online presence if you are interested in using social media for affiliate marketing. You have to be consistent by posting regularly and aiming to reach more people. If you do not post regularly, you may lose some followers as they may begin to lose interest if you are hardly ever online. People are only interested in following people who are regularly online as well as people who have interesting content. A very effective way to be successful in using social media for affiliate marketing is to carefully integrate your affiliate marketing strategies in your interesting and captivating content. You can use certain apps to make posts in advance while you get to dictate when they get published. Endeavour to respond when you get mentioned and when people reach out to you. Set some time out of your busy schedule to reach out to your followers or audience, answer their questions and make meaningful conversations with them.

CHAPTER TEN: KEYWORD RESEARCH IN AFFILIATE MARKETING

Keyword Research in Affiliate Marketing:

How do you use keyword research for affiliate marketing and how important is keyword research in affiliate marketing?

Using keyword research in affiliate marketing is a very crucial thing to do. This is what makes it really easy for your audience to find you. Finding your content organically is made really easy with proper Keyword research. When you invest your efforts and work really hard as an affiliate marketer, visibility is really important and one way to gain visibility is through proper keyword research. When you know the right words to use as well as how to fit them into your content properly, even when promoting your affiliate products on social media, it means you have secured your rightful place when it comes to getting found easily by your audience.

How can you come up with the right keywords?

You should first Know your niche: The first thing you want to do before commencing your keyword research journey is to first know your niche. You already know what your niche is. Just to remind you, your niche is the specific product you are willing to promote as well as the particular industry you really want to be in. To become effective at using your keywords, you have to stick to a particular keyword that defines your niche. This is how you become an expert at what you do and you become known for doing what you do. If you become an expert in a particular field, they can always trust your recommendations when it comes to such products. After finding a niche product, you can easily find deals with companies and brands looking for affiliate marketers to help drive sales and promote their brands. After finding a particular niche and brands you want to work with, this is when you can begin your keyword research. The niche you have carved for yourself goes a long way in determining what sort of audience you would be targeting. You must know the age range you are looking out for as well as the kind of interests that ought to be incorporated as well as other things that should be put in place. For example, if you will be focusing on a niche that has to do with baby cars, it means you will be looking out for parents and your keyword research should resonate with that and reach out to the right people. If your niche is men's wears, it means you will be targeting a different audience and will ensure your research is focused on various products. This is because you are looking out for the attention of a different type of audience.

Do your manual brainstorm: This is also one that is very effective in keyword research and it is the basis of your research. What do we mean by manual brainstorming? You have to rack your brain to come up with effective keywords for your affiliate marketing business. When you have the proper tools and the necessary things needed for an effective manual brainstorm, it becomes really easy to come up with unique keywords and effective ones, especially if you hit a mental roadblock. It is completely normal for you to be out of ideas, and there's nothing wrong in not knowing what to come up with. You can start from a particular foundation and try to work your way up from there. For example, you can try to sit down quietly and put yourself in the shoes of your audience. If you were in their shoes and you needed to find something about a particular keyword, what would you type? Asking yourself these types of questions helps you come up with reasonable keywords by getting into the mind of your audience and knowing what they would like. When you come up with these popular search items, you can be rest assured that your audience would want to use them when looking for the same information as well, you should fit them into your content in order to enhance visibility by your audience who want answers to their questions. They are people who are seeking great product recommendations when your keywords help them find a solution to their problems, they would definitely check you out.

You should create something from brainstorming manually: After you are done with your manual brainstorming, create a list of these broad-spectrum search terms you have been able to develop and make really specified keywords out of these widely-used ones. You can actually do this by visiting websites like Amazon, or other websites to make a research about your niche and see what people are saying about your niche in the other very similar keywords that come up when you search for these search terms. When you find these related keywords, you should include these terms to your list of previously brainstormed terms relating to your niche, in order to captivate your audience by ensuring that they are provided with the right products they are searching for. This is how you get to know what aspect of your niche product your audience find really intriguing. You can look for these seed type keywords by looking at great places on forums relating to your niche products and your target audience. You can also check websites designed for providing answers to questions asked by the general public. This is a great way to know what people are saying about your affiliate products and what they think about such products. You would know what intrigues them as well as what they are really inquisitive about. Knowing all these makes you ensure that your content is visible to your audience who are inquisitive and searching for answers. There are also several communities of affiliate marketers out there which affords you the opportunity to share information as well as useful sources that can help you become really successful.

You should ensure you keep up with the keywords: Do not forget to re-research your keywords sources regularly. These keywords seeds should be saved for the purpose of reference. The taste of your audience, as well as the styles used in affiliate marketing, seem to be really dynamic as they can change at any time. When you are always keeping up with these sources, they allow you to know what's trendy as well as what your audience seems to like, they also you're your audience find you when they need you at the moment and in the future, if you want to be successful as an affiliate marketer, you have to be consistent in your approach in order to be at the top of your game. This is because several things can go out of trend and you need to stay informed in order to ensure these changes are implemented in your strategies as an affiliate marketer. Keeping up with your keywords is a great way to be at the top of your game.

. . .

Never leave Intent out of the picture: When doing your keyword research, it is really essential to not leave Intent out of the picture. Instead of merely having social discussions about your niche or specific products and providing answers to the numerous questions of your audience, you need to pay attention to the "USER INTENT" when researching your keywords. Ensure that you provide the actual suggestions of your audience by knowing exactly what they intend to find. Make sure your affiliate links are effectively used when it comes to considering user intent, do not make use of ambiguous keywords and ensure that your keywords help your audience to find the right and exact product they really want.

Get rid of the really competitive keywords: When you have your endless lists of prospective keywords, you must ensure that you get rid of keywords that are really competitive if they would not give you an edge over your other competitions out there. You should aim to dominate in every niche you find yourself. The best way to do this is to ensure your keyword doesn't seem to be very competitive. If you want a chance to dominate, you must be really creative and unique in order to stand up and be easily found by your audience.

CHAPTER ELEVEN: MISTAKES YOU SHOULD NEVER MAKE AS AN AFFILIATE

There are several rookie affiliate marketing mistakes you really need to look out for as well as avoid. It would be in your best interest to ensure that these mistakes are carefully avoided. Some of these mistakes have caused several affiliate marketers so much, however, you don't need to worry. Knowing these things beforehand will definitely help you avoid these mistakes and will help you achieve success in your affiliate marketing business. Are you a beginner, who's simply thinking of joining the affiliate marketing industry and you don't want to make terrible mistakes? There's no cause for alarm, be rest assured that you are in safe hands. Maybe you have already commenced your journey as an affiliate marketer and you are really scared of making bloomers. Be rest assured that you will get the right knowledge you require to make it in the industry of affiliate marketing.

Here's a list of mistakes you really need to avoid making as an affiliate marketer:

Do not assume you can be a millionaire immediately: I keep stressing the fact that affiliate marketing isn't a get-rich scheme. However, you must know that there are so many misleading articles and blog posts on the internet that tell people that affiliate marketing can make you a millionaire in a couple of weeks or even weeks. You must know that these contents are nothing but embellished "nonsense" specially designed to confuse people or mislead them. Do not be deceived, no matter how excellently brilliant you may be as an affiliate marketer if you will become wealthy, it isn't something that happens in a twinkle of an eye. It is something that requires hard work, consistency and patience. There are several reasons why you cannot make instant wealth as an affiliate marketer. It is impossible to become immediately wealthy as an affiliate marketer because you don't have the proper connections, you barely have enough traffic, your contents are still very little and you haven't even built trust yet. If you can get rid of this misconception about getting rich really fast as an affiliate marketer, it will help you become really patient, hardworking and consistent in your business. What should you do to get rid of this mentality? In order to get rid of this mentality, you must learn to go at your own pace, give yourself time to grow by refusing to join every affiliate program that comes your way and by resisting the temptation to promote every expensive product out there. You need to make sure you pay attention to the more important things first. This isn't to say that you don't have to make money at all but the point is that you shouldn't make money your priority at the initial stage. The important things you need to concentrate on are; writing amazing content, driving traffic and getting enough emails.

Refusing to get enough emails at the beginning: This particular mistake is really common amongst the rookies in the affiliate marketing industry. We have all been there, every professional affiliate marketer has been through this phase before. Some people tend to postpone collection of emails until they are already in the industry for a couple of months or more. When you approach an expert and ask them what asset they find really important in their online business, I can assure you that the majority of them will tell you that it is a long list of email subscribers. Why Is it really important to build a long list of emails? It is really important for the following reasons:

It is an amazing way to build great traffic. Imagine having a list of very dedicated 2000 subscribers and you have recently published a very interesting 5,000-word article. The best way to create awareness about your recent article is to send them a mail. It is guaranteed that you will get at least 30% of these people to read your blog post and you can rest assured that more than half of them will post on their social media platforms. Remember how publicity can help your business grow. If anything happens to your ranking on Google, you still have your loyal email subscribers to fall back on. More subscribers mean more traffic for you and more sales for your affiliate products. This is why it would be a big mistake on your part to not build enough email list on time. It's never too early to start building your email list. You can do this by signing up for an email marketing service especially if the platform you are using is WordPress. There are a few services you could choose from. Some of the most popular ones you could choose from are Mail chimp (which is free for up to two thousand subscribers) You can change the services when you have more than 2000 subscribers. There is also AWEBER, this one offers you a 30-day free trial and begins at $19 per month for 500 subscribers. There is another popular one known as getting a response, this one begins at $15 every month and it is available for about 1500 subscribers. You can set up your account on any of these services but we will be using mail chimp for proper illustration.

Come up with a new list of email subscribers: The nest thing you need to do is to create a new email list. After this, you can Set up or upload an opt-in usage plugin: There are several WordPress opt-in form plugins to select from. You can choose from any of these.

Mail Chimp for WP – The Lite variety is unrestricted and stress-free. But there aren't really any customizable topographies

WP Subscribe –.

Mail Munch –

Optin Forms by Code Leon – This particular one's really amazing and it is completely affordable.

Never choose a niche you aren't interested in: If there is a mistake you would always live to regret as an affiliate marketer, it is the mistake of selecting a niche you are not passionate about at all. Why is it a grievous mistake to make? This is a very question that you need to pay attention to, especially as a newcomer in the affiliate marketing industry. It is a mistake you should avoid because the consequences are really obvious. You will never feel enthusiastic to write or talk about topics about your niche if you don't have a soft spot for your niche. Not choosing a niche you are passionate about will not make your niche a profitable one and going for a niche that isn't profitable is a disastrous decision to make. It's hard to keep up with a niche you do not find interesting, you are most likely going to end up not having contents to come up with and you will definitely give up on such niche.

. . .

How can you avoid making this mistake? You can avoid making this mistake by going for a niche you are really passionate about and by doing something that gives you fulfilment in order to avoid running out of ideas and things to say.

Avoid publishing unreadable content: Dear upcoming affiliate marketer, this is a mistake that has ruined the careers of so many affiliate markers and I'm sure you don't ever want to tread this path. How do you ever think of writing a product review that doesn't show your audience all they need to know and how to use the product effectively. You should learn how to write your content in such a way that it grabs the attention of your audience and makes them want to read. It doesn't have to be unnecessarily long but it should pass the right message across and tell your audience what you want to say in a method that isn't ambiguous at all. Ensure the content is humorous and relatable. Most people find the content they can relate to really captivating and interesting. In order to write such contents, you must motivate your audience by constructing your sentences carefully in such a way that it motivates your audience in an articulate and eloquent manner. You must pay attention to your language usage as well, ensure there is no grammatical blunder in your content and ensure it passes across your required message. You should try your best to ensure that you come up with ta op notch and high-quality content if you want to be successful as an affiliate marketer.

Deciding not to write product reviews: as an affiliate marketer, if you are not writing product reviews, you are missing out a great deal because most customers who search for product reviews are always ready to make purchases. You must also keep in mind that if you have an affiliate website, it would be best to write lots of product reviews in order to drive sales, traffic and conversion. How can you avoid making the mistake of not writing product reviews? You must ensure that you publish product reviews. You commence by selecting a product of your choice. Product reviews actually tell your audience what you feel about certain products. Do you think a product appears to be a scam? write a review to give your opinions and recommend other products they could purchase instead. Do you think the product is really amazing? You should write a product review about it, telling your audience why you should they should check it out and why you think it would benefit your audience. You can make your recommendations by pasting your affiliate links in the product review. You can check the internet to find products you would really like to review and recommend. Find these products by using the right keyword and by researching the product really well. Ensure that your review is completely honest, do not condemn another product because you want to recommend a particular one. You could get sued for publishing a false report about a brand or a product. You can come up with your template after doing your proper research. The next thing is to start writing exactly what you think about a product in clear terms, do not embellish or downplay a product but ensure your review is fun to read at the same time. Aim for at least one thousand words. The next thing you want to do is to optimize your product review for SEO. You can do this by using the right keywords, the right images and using the appropriates links. The next thing is to ensure your review is absolutely correct by proofreading, editing and then hitting the publish button.

Depending on google search traffic: One mistake you would make as an affiliate marketer is to depend heavily on google search traffic. Google would never rate a website that's only a few days old. It takes a lot to rank on Google's search result page and you shouldn't expect this to happen immediately. If your site is new, Google assumes you haven't gained visibility yet and you may not even be targeting the right keywords. You should use the right keywords, write quality contents and set your site up for SEO. You should also look for other sources of traffic for your affiliate marketing.

Do not flood your posts with affiliate links: Never make this mistake as you may get banned for spamming others with your affiliate links. You must develop strategic methods of placing your links as an affiliate marketer.

Promoting products with terrible reviews: This is a big mistake so many people make, even professional affiliate marketers still do this sometimes. If you are going all out for a product that has received several bad reviews, you are setting yourself up for a heartbreak because not only would you lose the trust of your audience, you will also realize that people would believe that every recommendation you give has something to do with the money you will be getting in return for recommending them. Ensure you have checked that a product has only fine reviews before recommending them, also endeavour to test a product before dishing out your recommendations to your unknowing audience. the last thing you want is to get called out for recommending a terrible product.

Not doing your work: So many affiliate marketers get tired when they do not get their desired result within a specific time. It's actually true that everything about affiliate marketing could get really overwhelming especially for beginners. You are not driving the sales you want and your traffic isn't really impressive too. I know that feeling and it's really not a good feeling. You may be tempted to give up on affiliate marketing and turn your back on the whole business but when you do that, you are going to be making a really huge mistake. How can you avoid making this mistake? You can avoid this mistake by ensuring that nothing else drives you but your passion for your niche and a motivation to succeed. With all these in mind, it would be difficult to abandon your work. Always keep in mind that these days when you aren't getting your desired results are the days of your early beginning and they should not be despised as they will set you up for the better future. When you get the urge to quit, you should wave it off and encourage yourself to do more instead and focus on building your business as an affiliate marketer.

Not allowing yourself to grow: This is a mistake you should never make as an affiliate marketer. There is a room for growth in every business you can actually think of. Do not assume you are already an expert after learning only a few things. You do not just become an expert overnight. There is a certain level of work you need to put in before you become really good at what you do. Allow yourself to learn so many things and learn from your superiors in the field before you start feeling like you know it all. Getting the right knowledge will set you up on your journey to becoming a professional affiliate marker but until then, you have to admit that you have so much to lean. You do not need to be shy about learning from people, remember that every expert out there actually started from somewhere.

. . .

Being in a rush to promote every expensive product that's out there: This is a mistake so many professionals in the field have made. If you are always in a rush to promote every expensive product that comes your way, you will be making a really big bloomer. It is definitely not the best thing to do because you will barely make any sales or make money. You need to understand that your product needs to cut across to a wide variety of audience because there are several people who don't have enough. You don't have to promote really expensive products before making it big in the industry. As long as you are making enough sales even when it comes to low-priced products, you can still make your money from the commission you get. How can you avoid making this mistake? You can avoid making this mistake by paying attention to the quality of a product first, before paying attention to the price. The quality of the product is the paramount thing.

Flooding your audience's Sidebars, Headers, and Footers with unnecessary Banner Ads: This mistake is one you really need to carefully avoid. You must have experienced this before, you want to read a post and you are being bombarded with unnecessary banner ads. The effect of this can be really annoying as you may even lose interest in the post itself. People could get easily irritated when this happens and they wouldn't hesitate to click the back button before you can say, Jack! Place your ads once in a while in a sidebar.

Promoting Products that aren't related to your niche: A lot of rookies in the field make this particular mistake of promoting products that are in no way related to your niche. You should never promote a product that has nothing to do with your niche. Your audience is following you and they are interested in your site for a particular reason. Digressing isn't the best thing to do, you need to stick to your niche if you do not want to bore your audience. Promoting other niche products will most likely make your audience lose interest and feel like they aren't getting what they really want. Imagine running a weight-loss niche and posting something about changing your flat tires.

Copying and pasting content from the products sales page: Most newbies or amateurs in the field do this a lot as a result of laziness. They are too lazy to come up with something creative and unique to put out there for their audience. This is why they take the easy way, they simply copy and paste. This is why I often encourage every beginner to find something passionate to talk about. This way, you find it really easy to come up with a creative and unique content You could even get penalized by Google for duplicating content and doing copy and paste. Always write your own content every time, instead of copying.

Not caring about your visitors: Never forget that your audience is human beings that should be paid some attention. Make sure you consider your visitors in anything you are doing as an affiliate marketer. If your website doesn't suit them or look really attractive, it would be really difficult to get them to come back. Ensure that your designs are captivating enough, they shouldn't be boring and they should be convenient and conducive for mobile-users. This basically means y0ou need to keep your audience in mind in whatever you do as an affiliate marketer.

SUMMARY

In this chapter, we talked about reasons so many affiliate marketers fail and how you need to look out for these mistakes and avoid making similar mistakes. The point of learning from people's mistakes is to make better choices than they ever did and to ensure that we become more successful.

Some of the mistakes we mentioned are:

Most affiliate marketers assume they are experts already. Without waiting to get all the knowledge required, some affiliate marketers often assume that they already know all there is to know already. They fail to ask questions and follow the footsteps of other successful affiliate marketers because they are too proud to ask for help. At the end of the day, they end up making little or no money at all. It is really necessary for you to ask for help and learn from your superiors. Remember that every expert was once an amateur. Give yourself a chance to grow by learning as much as you can and not giving up on acquiring knowledge.

Most affiliate marketers do what they do because of money: Money shouldn't be your only drive as an affiliate marketer because you have to consider so many other things. If money is your only drive as an affiliate marketer, you will be ruining a lot of things like the trust of your audience. Your priority should be your audience and not money. If you can do what your audience wants by ensuring that their safety comes first when recommending products, you will build trust and make some money as they begin to have faith in your recommendations.

Most people don't even know what they promote. Another thing we mentioned is the fact that some affiliate marketers hardly ever take out some time to research the product they are promoting and this is why so many of them fail. In order to They have no knowledge about the products they promote, in order to avoid making this mistake of recommending a product you barely know, you need to do your homework carefully to know what people are saying about the products. Check to ensure these products don't have bad reviews and also ensure that you test this product before recommending it to your audience. You should also ensure your product reviews promote nothing but honesty, say exactly what you think about a product without embellishing the truth or downplaying the quality of a product.

Most people simply go with the crowd. So many affiliate marketers are fond of doing copy and paste. They cannot come up with something unique and they are too lazy to be creative. It doesn't matter how new you are in the field, you need to ensure that you are not coping and pasting from the product's sales page. You can come up with something creative by ensuring that you are dealing with a niche you are very interested in. This is because there is creativity in passion and the most inspired people are passion-driven. If you want to original, you need to have adequate information about what you are talking about and this begins with choosing a niche you are familiar with.

So many people are quick to give up: Another mistake that many affiliate marketers make is the fact that they are very quick to give up when they aren't getting their desired result. In order to avoid making this mistake, you should never despise the days of your early beginning they set you up for greatness. Let consistency be your watchword and endeavour to stick to your passion even when you aren't getting what you want. Keep in mind, that everything will pay off one day and you will become someone who lends other people your knowledge in the field.

Most affiliate marketers actually forget to let their audience know where they stand. As an affiliate marketer, your target audience cherishes your recommendations and they trust in your advice. If they look up to you so much, you need to always let them know what your standpoint is. Are you for or against a product? Let these answers resonate through your product review and let your audience understand the point you are trying to drive at all times. How can you do this? You can do this by avoiding ambiguous messages and messages that aren't articulately expressed. Pay attention to your content and ensure it is topnotch. Never make this mistake and if you have ever done in the past, you should try your best not to ever repeat the same mistake in affiliate marketing as it kills your relationship with your audience.

Most people refuse to build their email list: Just as mentioned in this chapter, there are so many beginners in the affiliate marketing industry who refuse to build their email list because they think it is too early to do so. It is never too late to start building your email list, neither is it too early. You need to build your email list of loyal subscribers because they can help you drive more sales and more traffic. You can get at least 30% of your email subscribers to read your posts by notifying them just as soon as you write such posts. You can also be guaranteed that at least half of your total subscribers would share your post and help with publicity. You also get something to fall back on in case google does something funny.

. . .

Most people fail to put their audience first in what they do. As an affiliate marketer, you should never forget to put your audience first in whatever you do. Let your content solve the problems of your audience and ensure that your website isn't flooded with so many ad bars that could be a huge turn off for your audience.

CHAPTER TWELVE: HOW TO PROMOTE AFFILIATE MARKETING

All through the previous chapters, we have already stressed the fact that you need to work hard in order to make it as an affiliate marketer. However, in this chapter, we will be talking about how you can make so much from Affiliate marketing by doing the right thing. You need to know that so many people have made a lot from Affiliate marketing. How can you drive insane results as an affiliate marketer? You can be one of those people who are making so much from affiliate marketing. It all has to do with having the right strategies and possessing adequate knowledge. You can do this by promoting your affiliate links in the right way in order to grow your income. There's an opportunity for you in the industry despite the massive competition in the industry of affiliate marketing.

Do you want to learn how to promote your affiliate links, using the right platform? You need to pay attention to this chapter in order to get it the right way.

You already know that building passive income isn't as easy as so many people think. You need to be an active marketer and you must also be intentionally strategic, before reaching that stage where you sit on a couch far away in the city of your dream, while watching your money make itself even when you are fast asleep. Consider affiliate marketing as a way of building your brand. It's not just about building a website and sitting back. Having an online presence, getting interviewed on a podcast and even hosting your podcast, and guest posting for other people are ways to make it in the affiliate marketing industry. You should also endeavour to promote your content regularly. How do you get the attention of your audience and convert leads? You can do this by driving enough traffic.

How can you promote your affiliate links?

It might be frightening at the initial stage, but it's imperative to ensure that at least four or more strategies are combined for your affiliate products, instead of just paying attention to a particular strategy. This is because you cannot really get enough impact using only one strategy. You need to know that the amount of traffic you drive equals to your conversion rate as well as the leads you drive as well.

Do not just expect to promote your affiliate links without including noteworthy and convincing content when pasting your affiliate link. You need to know that it is essential to let your audience in, on all they need to know about a particular product when promoting it through your affiliate links. This process is known as using native ads.

. . .

What do we mean by native ads? These native ads are a way of advertising your affiliate products by ensuring that there is a level of consistency in the appearance, voice and the pattern of the platform you are making use of. So many affiliate marketers use this method of advertisement, which is hardly ever noticed by your audience as a means of advertisement. It is a natural method of advertising and promoting your affiliate products in such a way that your audience get carried away and get too interested to even notice it is an ad. Sounds great right? You can employ this strategy in promoting your affiliate link, it will definitely help generate more sales and traffic if it's catchy enough. Some affiliate marketers do this by using Instagram as a platform.

When you talk about your affiliate products, stating why you think the product is highly recommendable, paste your affiliate links alongside your content so that your audience can easily make a purchase.

It appears really easy to use an affiliate link and it isn't truly difficult. As long as you obey the laws and ensure that your audience is aware that these links are affiliate links. You must have seen certain posts on Instagram, especially if you are a regular user of Instagram, you must have noticed posts where an influencer or celebrity lets you know that they are being paid to promote a product. An example of this disclaimer is a post that shows something like "paid partnership" at the top.

You can promote your affiliate links by using your email list: You already know how essential it is to have an email list as an affiliate marketer. These are the people you can trust as they are your loyal subscribers. If they want your emails in your inbox, it means they trust you enough for that.

You can let your audience know about your affiliate products by sending them emails. This method is a great way of putting your link out there, to ensure that it reaches your target audience. It is a really personal way to communicate with your audience and you must make full use of it.

You can promote your affiliate link by using podcast: You can actually make thousands of dollars by using podcast to your advantage as an affiliate marketer. You can host your podcast and recommend certain products and tools to your audience. You can make your story more genuine and organic by ensuring that a story is built around your product.

You can promote your affiliate links by using videos: One great way to sell your affiliate product is to ensure that your audience sees the visual aspect of the products. You can do this when you practically show them how to use the product and by telling them about the product. Never underestimate the effect of using videos for the promotion of your affiliate links. It is easy to make videos and people are no longer interested in "telling", they want to see for themselves and confirm with their own eyes. This is why you really need to consider using videos as a means of promoting your affiliate links.

SUMMARY

CONCLUSION

Dear reader, thank you for buying this book. In a world which dominated by the use of "internet" and a world where business can hardly thrive, without having an online presence, affiliat marketing has become a trend and a great way to make mone

The idea of this book was conceived to help you explore the various ways to make money as an affiliate marketer and I ho you have learned how to be at the top of your game as a Topnc affiliate marketer. Cheers to bringing all your dreams to realit the affiliate marketing industry!

CPSIA information can be obtained
at www.ICGtesting.com
Printed in the USA
LVHW021533301020
670160LV00006B/816

CPSIA information can be obtained
at www.ICGtesting.com
Printed in the USA
LVHW021533301020
670160LV00006B/816

9 781648 086465

CONCLUSION

Dear reader, thank you for buying this book. In a world which is dominated by the use of "internet" and a world where businesses can hardly thrive, without having an online presence, affiliate marketing has become a trend and a great way to make money.

The idea of this book was conceived to help you explore the various ways to make money as an affiliate marketer and I hope you have learned how to be at the top of your game as a Topnotch affiliate marketer. Cheers to bringing all your dreams to reality in the affiliate marketing industry!

In this chapter, we learnt how to promote your affiliate links using several platforms as an affiliate marketer.

You can promote your links by using native ads which allows you to be really natural in your ads

You can also promote your links by using your email list of loyal subscribers who trust you enough to have your emails in their inbox.

Another way to promote your affiliate link is by employing the use of podcast.

You can also use videos as a visual presentation of how the product works and what the product looks like.